A Tear in the Curtain

A Tear in the Curtain

JOHN SYMONS

SHEPHEARD-WALWYN (PUBLISHERS) LTD

First published in 2013 by
Shepheard-Walwyn (Publishers) Ltd
107 Parkway House, Sheen Lane,
London SW14 8LS
www.shepheard-walwyn.co.uk
www.ethicaleconomics.org.uk

British Library Cataloguing in Publication Data
A catalogue record of this book
is available from the British Library.

ISBN: 978-0-85683-292-5

Typeset by Alacrity, Chesterfield, Sandford, Somerset
Printed and bound through
s|s|media limited, Rickmansworth, Hertfordshire

Dedicated to

Vladimir Bukovsky

with deep respect and admiration:
expelled from the Soviet Union after twelve years
in the GULAG Archipelago, 1977,
author of
To Build a Castle, 1978,
and
Moscow Trial, 1996,
Candidate in the Presidential election campaign
in Russia, 2007-2008

'Valiant for Truth'

This is the story of three families:

A Hungarian family
Tibor, Helena and Giori
And their mother Eva;

A Russian family
Andrei,
His parents Igor and Natalya
And his grandmother, 'Babushka',
and her friend Dmitry;
and
A British family
Margaret, her children Stephen and Elizabeth,
Her parents John and Barbara Durham,
And their Hungarian friends Geza and Miriam

Contents

August, 1991
Sussex

'MUM, what's happened to grandpa?' said Stephen. 'Come quickly!'

Margaret stopped making tea in her kitchen in Sussex and half ran into the sitting room. John Durham, her father, was there watching the television. The screen showed an immense crowd of people in front of a white office building beside the Moscow River.

A tall, stocky man with thick white hair stood high on a tank facing the crowd. Two other men stood on either side of him. They were holding up makeshift armour to protect him from snipers' bullets.

The man, Boris Yeltsin, the President of Russia, was saying, '*Demokratiya pridyot*', 'Democracy will come'. The crowd cheered back, '*Ro-ss-i-ya*', 'Russia', 'Yeltsin, Yeltsin!'

Tears were pouring down Mr Durham's face. On his knee was a black and white photograph, taken thirty-five years ago, of Margaret and three of her friends, all shivering, in swimming suits on the beach at Woody Bay, with the cliffs behind them. One of them Stephen could just recognise as his Aunt Helena.

'Is Grandpa all right, Mum?' Stephen asked.

And turning to his mother, he saw that she, too, was sobbing, as she went over and threw her arms around her father.

Day after day that week Stephen sat on the sofa alongside his grandfather and his mother watching television reports from Moscow. He and his sister, Elizabeth, two years younger than him, did a lot of the shopping and cooking so Mum and Grandpa could watch everything as it happened. John and Margaret also listened hour after hour to radio broadcasts, in Russian, from Moscow. They saw on the television screen events no one had predicted: the collapse of the Communist Party of the Soviet Union; the locking and sealing of all its offices across a vast country; the seizure, by President Yeltsin's new Russian government, of all the records of the Party's countless crimes against Russians and foreigners; and the return to Moscow of Mr Gorbachev, President of the dying Soviet Union, from his holiday home on the coast of the Black Sea where, he said, he had been held captive by his subordinates in the Communist Party.

One evening in Moscow a crane was brought into Lubyanka Square. It toppled from its tall, granite pedestal the statue of the first head of Lenin's infamous secret police, the Cheka, set up in 1917. Impotent for the moment, Officers of the KGB, the hated successor of the Cheka, watched what was happening from their dark offices on the Square. Countless innocent people had been tortured and shot in the cellars of that building.

Statues of Lenin himself, the begetter of the Russian Civil War and of all the terrors and famines of the past seventy-five years, crashed down in front of crowds all over the country. Russians were rejoicing as they seized the chance to free themselves; it might never come again. How long freedom would last no one knew, but it was to be used to the full as long as they had it.

And all week Stephen and Elizabeth's grandfather John and mother Margaret kept looking at the old photograph.

'Tibor,' said John, 'if only Tibor...'

'Whatever will Helena be thinking? And Andrei...'

'Perhaps we'll find out at last what happened to him.'

For them this snap was now an icon. Somehow, although John had taken such care of it over the years, it was creased. When the light played on it, it seemed that the gap that had at one time kept Andrei apart from the others had been removed, and all four of them were held in one embrace.

1956
Woody Bay

'ONE more swim,' said Tibor, *'please.'*

It had been a long day on the beach at Woody Bay. By now the Durham family were the only people left there. The tide was going out quickly, leaving a stretch of smooth clean sand, cool after the afternoon's heat. All the picnic food was long since eaten.

'All right, one more,' said John Durham.

'Just one,' added his wife, Barbara.

'Thank you.' Andrei's English had hardly a trace of a Russian accent. 'Thank you.'

Cheering and shouting in a mixture of English and Hungarian, Tibor raced into the water, followed by his sister Helena, and after them Andrei and Margaret. Tibor's Hungarian changed into Russian as he kicked up the waves to splash Andrei and the others.

They all struck out, swimming quickly across the bay and back, not talking now but grunting and groaning from their efforts. As usual, Tibor won the race. He was four years older than the others, strong and fit.

They all pounded up the beach, Tibor again leading the way, eager now to get back to the caravan for fish and chips, to be followed by tinned pears and custard, and cocoa. Barbara gave them their towels. As they rubbed off the water, John called them into a line and took a photograph, the last photograph after the last swim of that year's holiday. No more swims in 1956.

When she saw the photograph later Barbara was surprised that John had managed not to cut off their heads or their feet. It was a good photograph. Tibor stood on the left, tall with dark straight hair and a dark complexion, almost blackened by the unexpectedly strong sun during his two weeks in England. He had his arm around Helena protectively, although she wanted no protection; also dark, but with startling pale eyes, she was looking through the camera, through John Durham, to something beyond this holiday. Margaret stood next to her. Each of the two girls had an arm around the other's shoulder, laughing and shivering, for by now it was turning cool. Margaret was fair, and pink from the sun, although the black and white photograph (to her pleasure, when she saw it) disguised this. Then there was a gap, and Andrei stood awkwardly, a little nervous, with fair hair, thin, a narrow face; half mild, half severe; half frowning, half smiling, with his towel around his shoulders. And, behind them all, the smooth slate cliffs rose two hundred feet in the evening sun.

John arrived back at the caravan, bent over a little by the weight of a tall enamel jug of water, fresh from the stand-pipe shared by all the families on the site. He heaved it up to put down heavily on the old table outside the caravan.

In those days in the Fifties no road went down to Woody Bay and there were few cars on the roads anyway. Families walked to the beach on a footpath which ran for a mile, by a little stream, down the combe from the village where the bus stopped. There was a tiny caravan site for a few holiday-makers.

Barbara was standing inside the caravan as John arrived, with the bread knife in her hand, listening to the old black portable radio on the table.

'I have always been a man of peace,' said a voice, rather silky, the voice of the Prime Minister, Sir Anthony Eden. 'I could not be anything else if I wished to be. I was a League of Nations man; a United Nations man.' But the Prime Minister went on to speak with foreboding of the danger of a war between Britain and Egypt.

Mr Durham turned off the radio as the young people arrived, dressed and ready to eat. This was not an evening to be overshadowed by fear of war.

At his school John Durham taught French and German, but that did not explain how Tibor and Helena, from Hungary, and Andrei, from Russia, came to be spending two weeks in England that summer, first at school and then on holiday at the seaside.

John's deepest love was for the two languages that he knew even better but he did not teach, Russian and Hungarian. He had learnt them thoroughly, twelve years ago, in Army Nissen huts. The Second World War was drawing to its end. Within eighteen months Germany's downfall would be complete and Hitler would be dead.

'If you don't keep up and pass the tests each week, back you go to basic training,' the students were told. No one on John's course had to go back.

After training John was sent with a special unit to Austria. Although he was only twenty-two years old, his job was to interview dozens of Hungarians and Russians who were trying to emigrate to Western Europe or America before the Soviet Union could freeze the borders and imprison them. He had to deal with the Soviet officials who were demanding that none of their citizens should be allowed to stay in the West. He interviewed Russians two or three times as old as himself.

'Find some loophole,' they pleaded. 'Help us to stay here.'

But Stalin, the Soviet dictator, was so strong that he forced Mr Churchill and President Roosevelt to send all Russians and other Soviet citizens back to him. His Red Army had fought its way first to Berlin, far ahead of Great Britain and the United States. Backed by an enormous force of arms, Stalin could demand and get whatever he wanted. What Stalin demanded was merciless. There was no hope that at home these poor displaced Russians would be spared execution or the labour camps which they knew awaited them. Stalin treated as traitors or spies all those who had been taken prisoner by the Germans in the War.

John loved the languages, but he loathed the events which he was witnessing. He was shocked by the despair in the eyes of an elderly Russian couple. Only their sense of dignity held them back from throwing themselves on the bare wooden floor in front of him, to beg to be allowed to go to Paris where so many Russian refugees had settled after the Bolsheviks seized power in 1917.

John felt somehow ashamed and guilty when others were reduced to obvious lies and wheedling, although all their efforts were destined to fail. He hated to refuse a safe escape to Hungarians who had so much in common with the Austrians among whom he was working in Vienna. He despaired at the finality of the decisions to be recorded on files, decisions which often meant death. He was glad that he was an interpreter and that his seniors had to take the decisions which led to British soldiers, against their will, forcing Russians into trains going east to Russia.

In September 1945, three months after he was 'demobbed' from the Army, John and Barbara, got married. In October they went to Oxford, and John began a special two-year degree course for ex-servicemen. They had known each other from primary school. Two years later, with their baby, Margaret, they settled down in Battle in Sussex.

John was a born teacher but the work somehow did not completely satisfy him. He was still pursued by memories and sometimes by nightmares. When she was feeding Margaret in the middle of the night, Barbara would sometimes hear John cry out when he was dreaming about people whom he had interviewed and who might well have died in Russia or Hungary. He would get up and sit with Barbara and Margaret for a while.

For a few years there was almost no news except the threat of war. An Iron Curtain descended in Europe, dividing East from West, from the Baltic Sea to the Adriatic, just as Mr Churchill had said in his famous speech in 1946 on a visit to the United States as the guest of President Truman.

Then, in 1949, the Communists in China, supported by Stalin, took power. Everywhere Stalin poured out his gold to Communist Parties, and he backed and encouraged armed groups to extend Soviet power, *his* power, in many countries. He used a war in Korea as a trial run for an attack on Japan, a far greater prize.

But before that attack could take place Stalin died in 1953. Although many people in Russia wept at the news of his death, they soon dried their tears. Millions of people were gradually released from the prison camps which were spread through that boundless land 'like an archipelago of countless islands'. Coming home, they told their families many truths. Under

Stalin's successors, tension eased between East and West.

So it was that, in 1955, John Durham persuaded his school to make a small exchange of students with Russia and Hungary. The headmaster was reluctant.

'It can't be done,' he said.

The head's pessimism seemed to be justified as the difficulties multiplied. But John was determined.

'We must try. We owe it to them to make the effort. They didn't want to be cut off behind Stalin's Iron Curtain.'

John persuaded the headmaster. His persistence paid off. With the unofficial help of a diplomat in the Foreign Office whom John knew from their days in the Army together, and an association of Russian Teachers, two very small groups of Russian and Hungarian children arrived at Liverpool Street Station in London in July 1955. They came with a few teachers and guides who were at first stiff and stern. But when they travelled out into the Sussex countryside with John and left behind the suspicious men from the Soviet and Hungarian Embassies who had been at the station to meet them, the teachers, like the children, began to relax.

For a week the foreigners lived with English families and visited their schools. The visitors, although carefully chosen and able to speak clear and fluent English, were thin and pinched by their harsh life.

The visit was a success, and it was repeated the following year. The same teachers returned with new groups of children. Tibor, Helena and Andrei were

18

among them. There was a less troubled air about the visitors, as if something was improving at home, giving more hope for the future. The Hungarians, especially Tibor, were reserved with the Russians. Tibor was proud of his country, so much smaller than the Soviet Union. He avoided speaking Russian as much as possible although all Hungarian children learnt it intensively at school. But even Tibor's tension relaxed in the second week of the visit. After school broke up, the Durhams took Tibor, Helena and Andrei with Margaret to Woody Bay.

'We love it there,' Margaret explained. 'We go there every summer holiday. It's my favourite place in the world.'

Tibor and Helena had swum in Lake Balaton in Hungary; and Andrei had swum in rivers and lakes in Russia. But to swim in the sea was new to all three of them.

Tibor and Helena, Andrei and Margaret swam and rowed boats and fished. They walked over the cliffs on footpaths clouded with butterflies and listened to skylarks in the fields. In the dusk they lay in the tough, long grass that grew by the seaside and watched the first stars appear. They saw the enchanting green light of glow-worms in the hedges. They were the last to leave the sea in the evening, and the first to run into it the next morning.

After their first swim each day they went to buy the bread and milk and a newspaper at the small shop. The site held a dozen caravans. In the village there was only Mr Crooks' shop, the post office and a telephone box. On Friday evenings a van came to sell fish and chips, a final treat before families left at the end of their holiday.

'It's a simple life,' said John.

'The best of all lives,' Andrei replied, the first time that he had spoken up like that. Tibor and Helena agreed. Margaret flushed and looked very pleased.

John and Barbara sat, one at each end of the table, with the four young people between them.

Barbara divided the steaming hot fish and chips on plates already warmed in the calor gas oven. She put on the table bread and butter, and mugs with steaming cocoa to comfort them after the cold of their last long swim. There was a basket overflowing with ripe plums.

'Here's a big piece of cod for you, Tibor... and for you Andrei, because you've got an even longer journey home.'

They were all yawning, exhausted by the day's exercise and the sea air, and went to bed early. John and Barbara listened to the news on the radio before they turned in. The inside of the caravan glowed cosily in the friendly silver light cast by the mantles of the calor gas lamps, but the news was not good. Britain and France were threatening action if President Nasser of Egypt went ahead with his policy to control the Suez Canal. There was a short item about tension in Hungary, and a demonstration there by students in

Budapest and other cities against the Soviet Union's domination of their country.

John and Barbara did not sleep well that night for fear of what awaited their new friends in the weeks to come.

'It reminds me of those nights when you woke up because of bad dreams and came to join me when I was feeding Margaret. How long ago that seems.'

'Perhaps the world is changing less than we hoped,' John replied.

Next morning, submerged by their luggage, they all set off for home in a green Morris Oxford motor car that had belonged to John's parents in the 1930s.

Sussex and London

'WE'RE going to be late.' Andrei's face was pale and tense, so different from two days ago at Woody Bay. 'We mustn't be late. It would be bad, bad for my family.'

All six of them were on the train from Battle to Charing Cross station in London. Andrei had been nervous all morning. When she saw his anxious expression at breakfast Barbara was sure that he had not slept.

He had packed his suitcase neatly, putting in it the smart, green pullover that the Durhams had given him. They were afraid that Andrei might not wear it back in Moscow. His parents might not wish him to draw attention to himself by wearing something so foreign.

'We'll give it to him, just like the others,' Barbara suggested to John. 'His parents can decide what to do.'

Andrei had not spoken to them much about his family and they had been careful not to ask him many questions.

Tibor looked anxious, too, but was too proud to confess it.

'No, it's a good train Andrei,' said Margaret. 'We're

never late. We go up to London on it for the pantomime every year after Christmas.'

Helena began to talk to Margaret about the performances she and Tibor had seen in the special children's theatres and circuses in Budapest, but at the New Year, not at Christmas.

Andrei explained about 'Grandfather Frost', who brought children New Year presents when the snow lay on the streets, almost undisturbed by traffic.

'It's so cold that drops of moisture freeze in your nose and it tingles,' he told Margaret.

'The winter comes quickly. By the beginning of October the leaves are gone from the trees and we have our first real frosts. Severe frosts and snow can come in November. We Russians love our winters.'

'We used to love Christmas in Budapest until the Russian Army came,' said Tibor quietly, almost speaking to himself. He was the only one of the four who could remember anything at all of the years before 1945. He had been three years old when the Red Army had swept over Eastern Europe into Hungary, pushing the Nazis before them back into Germany until they captured Berlin and raised the red Soviet flag with its hammer and sickle on the roof of the German parliament building.

Tibor and Helena did not know how it had happened, but their father had been killed as the Soviet Army forced its way through Hungary. He had never seen Helena, who was born seven months after his death. Tibor imagined that his father had been a hero, fighting both the Nazis and the Soviet Army, but their mother never spoke of it. There was so much that it was not safe to talk about. From their earliest days Tibor and Helena had sensed this and conformed. Something about their mother, her tension or a frown, always told them when they were approaching dangerous topics. It became second nature to everyone in Hungary, and Tibor quickly learnt the new rules.

The new rules permitted barely a mention of Christmas as it had been in the old days, although Tibor's first memory was of church at Christmas. His mother and father had taken him, only three years old, to the midnight service on Christmas Eve. He remembered being taken from cold, frightening streets into a warm candle-lit church, with the smell of a Christmas tree and incense. The Red Army was stalking those streets within a few weeks of the Nazis' flight. Christmas was also gone, and with it his father.

'It was a happy time,' said Tibor.

Andrei looked away.

Tibor regretted what he had said. He liked Andrei, and it was not his fault that he had lost his father and the old happy days. He felt that Andrei and his parents, too, had been the victims of some disaster, and that he and Helena had much in common with him.

'Look, Tower Bridge, Andrei. Don't worry. We'll soon be there.' Margaret pointed towards the Thames.

'Too soon,' said Andrei, perversely. They all laughed.

After London Bridge station the train started and stopped time and again as it made its way through a bottleneck, where six lines became four, to Waterloo East, and over the River to Charing Cross station. It stood for a couple of minutes on Hungerford Bridge. In clear sunlight everyone could see Big Ben and the Houses of Parliament, up river to the west. As Big Ben struck, the train rattled into Charing Cross, on time.

As John and Barbara shepherded everyone away to get a taxi, crowds of people struggled to get their luggage together on the platform to board the train. It was still the school holidays. Families from London were keen to get away to Hastings and other south coast resorts. Not trusting the fine weather many of the men and women were wearing raincoats and hats; the boys wore shirts and shorts, the girls dresses and sandals.

There was an atmosphere of cheerful excitement, held in check by the feeling families had that they were somehow on show. Clouds of tobacco smoke billowed from the fathers' cigarettes and pipes. Families seemed to feel shy with each other as this annual holiday ritual threw them together closely for a week or fortnight. The fathers found it difficult, so used were they to exile from their family at the office or factory five and a half days a week. When the men travelled by train it was usually on the way to or from work, with newspapers to read and hide behind, not with wives and children; and in a soulless silence, not in a cheerful buzz.

John looked at them. How lucky he was that his work in the school did not isolate him from his family. He was looking forward to Margaret's joining the first form of his school in a few weeks' time.

The six of them squeezed into a black taxi; it took them swiftly across London towards the Hungarian and Russian Consulates. There was not much traffic, but the driver complained about what there was.

The cab was to drop Barbara with Tibor and Helena at the Hungarian offices. As it pulled into the kerb three large Army lorries, painted in light sandy colours for desert camouflage, passed them, belching black and blue exhaust fumes. The soldiers on board were only three or four years older than Tibor, national servicemen doing their two years' compulsory military training. They looked puzzled, as if they could not believe what was happening to them. The drivers and the sergeants, some of them much older men who had taken part in the Second World War, knew what was happening but they also looked incredulous. Was it coming to this again so soon, when it seemed they had only just got used to peace? Were they going to have to fight in the deserts of North Africa from which they or their brothers and fathers had driven Field Marshal Rommel and the German troops only fourteen years earlier?

'On the way to the docks to embark for the Mediterranean and head for Egypt,' John muttered to Barbara. They felt thankful that no one in their family was directly involved.

As they stood rather stiffly on the pavement in front of the Hungarian Consulate, Margaret hugged Tibor and Helena. Barbara and John kissed Helena. Tibor shook hands with John; he clicked his heels, bowed and kissed Barbara's hand.

'Next year, at Woody Bay,' said Barbara.

'Next year,' said Helena enthusiastically.

'For ever and ever,' said Andrei, standing quietly at the edge of the group. He blushed and looked down at his feet.

They all laughed.

On an impulse Helena embraced Andrei.

Tibor shook Andrei's hand. 'I'm sorry about what I said on the train.'

Andrei quietly returned his smile and nodded. He waved to all the others as he got back into the taxi with John and Margaret to drive on to the Soviet Embassy.

Barbara took Tibor and Helena inside to join the rest of the exchange students, already gathered in a reception hall on the ground floor of the embassy. The group's leader and the Hungarian Consul were there. It was a bare, echoing room: a high ceiling, faded curtains and wall-paper, immense central heating pipes and radiators, a smell of stale, rough tobacco, and a dusty carpet. The pupils stood there, huddled together and swallowed up by the room, impersonal and indifferent to them all.

'Good morning, Mrs Durham,' said the Consul. Gold teeth flashed for a moment, the smile of a shark, as he looked coldly at her. He was a tall man in a shiny blue suit with receding hair, slicked back with Brylcream.

Barbara shook hands with him and moved on quickly to talk to Monika, the group's leader. She taught English in Budapest. The previous year she had been very nervous but had relaxed when she had a long conversation with John at the end of that visit. She smiled shyly at Barbara and welcomed back Tibor and Helena. They said a final goodbye to Barbara and joined their group.

In the hubbub the Consul's attention was distracted as he tried to sort out some papers and lists of names.

Monika had a chance to turn to Barbara. 'How is John? I am sorry not to see him.'

Barbara told her about the holiday and about Andrei. She explained that John was taking him back to join the Russian group. 'He is sorry not to see you.'

'There may be no chance next year,' Monika said, looking troubled. 'Things may not be easy for us when we get home. The sooner we get there the better.'

She gestured towards the door and together she and Barbara walked out of the Embassy. Barbara received another cold smile from the Consul.

On the steps outside, away from the Consul's view, Monika embraced Barbara for a moment.

An Army lorry, again in sandy camouflage colours, groaned past the end of the street on its way to the docks.

'This will be bad for us,' said Monika. 'If you try to stop Nasser seizing the Suez Canal...

'President Eisenhower has already said that force must not be used against Nasser and that America will not support any military action. And if America and Great Britain are at odds and distracted, the Soviet Union can do what it likes to us. We are such a small people and we have such hopes now for greater freedom.'

'What...?'

'The Russians will simply invade our country. Invasion, simply invasion... Our young people are in turmoil. In my school Tibor and his friends are excited by what their older brothers and sisters are saying and doing at the university. Even the lecturers there are speaking openly. They want freedom to form other political parties, separate from the Communist party, as the Austrians can do.'

'... Just over the border,' said Barbara.

'... Just across the border,' Monika nodded. 'Even some officials in the Communist Party say they want change. A few of them seem to know that their power is based on nothing but lies and the force of arms. Some people want us to break away from the Soviet Union and join NATO.

'Russia will never let us do that. And if you and the Americans fall out, what hopes are there for a tiny country like ours?'

Another Army lorry roared past the end of the street.

Monika sighed deeply. She suddenly stood erect and tense as the Consul came out to find her.

'I was worried about losing you, Mrs Kodaly,' he said sourly.

Monika shook hands formally with Barbara who turned away slowly. On the spur of the moment she decided to walk back through Green Park and then St James' Park to Charing Cross station so as to give herself a chance to think about it all.

At the Soviet Consulate John and Margaret waited with Andrei. A few other exchange students arrived with the teacher who had been their host. Margaret was the only English person there as young as the Russian visitors.

Two Russian officials gave them a cup of tea with a slice of lemon and a few cubes of sugar. Margaret did not enjoy the tea, but was interested to sit in the reception room. There was a bust of Lenin on the mantelpiece and a light patch on the wall above his grey metallic head where a portrait of Stalin had hung for many years. No picture had yet replaced his because an obscure power struggle was in progress in the Kremlin. Nikita Khrushchev, who had led the condemnation of Stalin in February that year, was emerging as its victor. Quite soon his portrait would take its place above Lenin's bust.

'I hope that it will be possible to welcome some Russian pupils again next year,' John said to the cultural attaché.

'It will not be possible if you indulge in imperialist adventures in Egypt against President Nasser,' he replied.

The attaché was severe and unsmiling. The previous

year when relations had been improving between Great Britain and the Soviet Union he had been friendlier.

John did not reply. Instead, he told the attaché that Andrei had played an active part in the exchange at school and had been a good guest on holiday.

Andrei looked worried, fidgeting and shifting from foot to foot. He wanted Mr Durham and Margaret to leave as quickly as possible. At the front door, as he shook John's hand, he looked him in the eye and mouthed the words 'For ever and ever' and smiled broadly. For a moment his face was transformed, almost lighting up the hall. In the confused comings and goings no one but John and Margaret could have seen it. They smiled at him and both nodded, and then walked away.

A little way down the street they turned to wave. Andrei had disappeared.

London

THE Durhams met at St James's Park underground station and waited on the platform for the train to Charing Cross.

Margaret felt worried. 'I didn't like it in that Consulate. The Soviet Consul and that Attaché gave me the creeps. Something's wrong there.'

'It was bad at the Hungarian office, too,' Barbara agreed.

'There was a smell of fear. They are unhappy places. And Helena and Tibor and Andrei have to go back there. Will we ever see the three of them again?'

On the platform some people were carrying furled banners. There was a demonstration planned for Trafalgar Square that afternoon, to protest at the government's policy over Suez.

'And why did Andrei change like that? It's been happening since we got back from the caravan. Tibor and Helena changed a bit, too. But Tibor's so proud that he didn't want to let me see it. Helena can't pretend.'

'They had to start getting ready for what it's like at home,' John replied. 'They have to fit in there.'

'Well, there's something wrong there, then,' said

Margaret. 'Why did Andrei say it would be bad for his family if he got to the Embassy late?'

'It's much worse in Russia than in Hungary,' John told her. 'And the rules can be changed suddenly. You saw that mark on the wall where Stalin's portrait had hung for so long... So much has changed in the last three years. I never dreamed, before *he* died, that we would ever be able to have an exchange of a few pupils and teachers like this. I think that they allowed it as some sort of experiment for some reason.'

'But will they be all right?' Margaret asked. 'Will it get worse if we have a war with Egypt, as that awful diplomat told you? I want them all to come again next summer.'

'So do I,' said John. 'And I want others to be able to come. The teachers seemed keen for that when they were on their own with me.'

The smell of fear had reminded John of the Russians and Hungarians whom he had had to interview eleven years earlier. What they still feared, he thought, was returning to the mercy of people like that Soviet diplomat, knowing that there would be no mercy in that system.

'Let's have a sandwich,' suggested Barbara.

They found a cafe by the River Thames on the Embankment. To distract themselves at the end of their holiday and the finality of the goodbyes, they went to the cinema near Piccadilly Circus. They joined the queue for the afternoon performance of *A Town like Alice*.

Leaving the cinema, the Durhams walked down the Haymarket into Pall Mall, and turned towards Charing Cross. They were planning to have tea at Lyons Corner House opposite the station before going home.

They walked past the line of stumpy fig trees, with their enormous green leaves, trained up against the blackened walls of the National Gallery. Pruned severely every year, the trees were doomed never to fruit.

There was a murmur like the sound of a swarm of angry bees, rising from the crowd filling the Square, between the majestic statues of lions and the fountains.

'This is where those people with banners were coming,' said Margaret. She read the slogans stretched out above the heads of the crowd, turned towards a makeshift platform.

A voice floated across to them, reinforced by a loud-speaker and echoing back from the buildings around the Square.

'Sir Anthony Eden is too *stooo-pid* to be Prime Minister,' said the voice.

It was a smooth voice, with a silky sheen to it, like that of Eden himself which Margaret had heard on the radio at the caravan. It was hypnotic, serpentine, rising and falling as it tried to conceal a stammer, almost singing while it played the crowd like a musical instrument.

'There is nothing left for the government but to get out – *get out* – *get out*,' crooned the voice, and the crowd roared back its approval.

Margaret could just see the man with the voice. He was wearing a suit, with a waistcoat and a watch-chain; she saw it glint as he turned from side to side to address the crowd. He had black hair, going grey in places, thick, with a careful parting, and the swagger and strut of a magpie. His face was a little lopsided, but when he spoke it was as if an electric current ran from him to the crowd and back again.

Margaret was not sure that she liked what was happening. She felt a sort of fear, nothing like as bad as the atmosphere back in the room in the Soviet Consulate. But somehow she knew that, if he spoke long enough, that man could make a crowd do whatever he wanted even if the individuals in it half-knew that they would come to regret it the next day.

John took Barbara and Margaret firmly by the arm on either side of him and forged ahead across the road to South Africa House, opposite St Martins-in-the-Fields church. In the Corner House there was a comforting smell of toast and tea cakes, a hiss of steam, and tables with check cloths and wooden chairs.

'I'm not sure whether I liked the man with the voice,' Margaret said. 'There was a sort of spell in his voice. Did he really expect the government to get out?'

'He's a mixed bag,' said John.

'Who is he?' Margaret asked.

'Mr Aneurin Bev*an*, not to be confused with Mr Ernest Bev*in*,' said Mum. 'Aneurin, but they call him *Nye*.'

'He might persuade you to do something you would be ashamed of later.' Margaret had become thoughtful.

'Not at all like Mr Bev*in,*' said Dad. 'Ernie Bevin... You knew where you were with him. He'd started life as a plough-boy on a farm in Somerset and ended up as Foreign Secretary. He and Mr Attlee set up the North Atlantic Alliance with the Americans to protect us and Western Europe from Stalin.'

'It really did save us,' said Mum.

'I always remember what Nye Bevan said in 1942,' said Dad.

'Here we go,' Mum smiled.

'... Well, I was eighteen in 1942,' said Dad. 'Nye Bevan was already an MP, very cocky and big-headed. He was a thorn in the side of Mr Churchill when he was trying to save us from Hitler...'

'... A cheek it was, too,' Mum said, 'Because all the years before the war Bevan and his crew had worked to stop us re-arming against Germany. They only got really keen on the war when Hitler attacked Russia in June 1941.'

'Nye Bevan had the nerve to say in the House of Commons* that the British people had more confidence in the sagacity of the Russian Generals Voroshilov and Timoshenko than they did in Mr Churchill. I was only eighteen, but what he said made me furious. Stalin and those generals had been Hitler's allies against us until fifteen months before

* See *Speeches of Aneurin Bevan at Westminster*, Volume 1, page 111.

that, crushing Poland and Eastern Europe, and sending Hitler oil and iron and food, everything the Germans needed. Stalin spent most of the 1920s and 1930s training Germany's air force and army. He only changed sides when Hitler suddenly went mad and attacked him... Since then I've never trusted Bevan or believed a word he says.'

Mother was ordering tea and teacakes.

'Someone has to be practical and feed your great brains,' she said.

A waitress in a starched, stiff dress and apron brought a brown pot of tea, a jug of hot water and another of milk. She gave each of them a cream-coloured plate with a toasted teacake, sliced open and moist with butter, or was it margarine? Margaret did not care. The warmth, the food and the talk comforted her after a long day.

They all went home in the train, content.

Only as Margaret lay in her bed that night did she think again of the goodbyes, picturing Tibor, Helena and Andrei and wondering what awaited them at the end of their journey home across the Continent.

Hungary

TIBOR and Helena stood in the square in front of Kaleti railway station in Budapest, swamped by a mass of travellers. They had made their way by train across Europe to Vienna where they had changed for the last hundred miles of the journey.

Crossing Vienna, they saw sights and people not all that different from what they had left behind in Budapest a fortnight earlier. Stocky men and women, like the Hungarians, but bustling about with a vibrant sense of purpose and looking much better fed.

They smelt the same smells of strong coffee and of pork being cooked with dumplings. In the restaurant at the station in Vienna the food was abundant and the china and table cloths were bright and new, but Austrian prices were far out of their reach.

Although they were on their way home and longing to see Mother, it somehow felt more difficult to be returning than to be going the other way at the start of their holiday. It made them sad to think that.

'We must be careful what we say to Mother and Giori,' said Helena.

'It was almost too good to be true in England, but it was true. We were so lucky. If we feel like this, what's it like for Andrei?' The talk on the train on the way from Battle to Charing Cross had made Tibor realise what life must be like for Andrei in Moscow.

At Kaleti station they felt tension in the air. There may have been more policemen and soldiers than when they had left for England, but perhaps that was just their imagination.

'Things have moved on,' said Tibor, nodding towards the armed policemen. 'I've missed a lot in two weeks.'

'Don't...' said Helena, but as she spoke Giori, their brother, came up to them. He was two years older than Helena, and two younger than Tibor. He had been happy to stay at home and to take care of Mother while they had been away.

'Welcome home. We've missed you both.' Giori took Helena's case. He was more placid than Tibor, less independent than Helena. There was something calm and steady in him. He seemed to have a strong sense of responsibility, a streak of realism.

With Helena between them, and weighed down by their luggage, Tibor and Giori struggled through the mass of people in front of the station. They crossed the square and caught a tram to their flat in an old building, not far from the centre of the town.

In the stone façade of their block there were still deep jagged holes left by the gunfire exchanged by the Soviet Army and the retreating Nazi troops twelve years ago.

The three of them trudged up the stairs and Mother welcomed them home with a special tea. She and Giori had as much to tell Tibor and Helena as they had to say about their time in England.

Russia

ANDREI's family lived in a block of flats near the centre of Moscow, but he did not go there on his return from England.

His parents, Natalya and Igor, were allocated a small dacha, a summer house built of wood, in the country seventy miles north of the city. It was here that Andrei spent the eight weeks of the school holidays in the summer with his mother and his father's mother, Ludmila. Andrei called her 'Babushka'.

Igor worked at a university institute in Moscow. He spent his week editing the texts of ancient Russian poems and stories and teaching university students. He used to come to join his family at weekends. Natalya worked there as a translator of English books.

The dacha was set in a large plot of land. The family could use it only in the short, hot Russian summer. Each autumn they carefully closed it up, sealing the windows and doors, to keep it safe through the next six months. Winter came early. There could be sharp frosts even in September. Before the frosts arrived it was necessary to harvest the crops: potatoes, beetroot, cabbages and onions, apples and plums; and the seeds of flowers to plant next spring.

By the time Andrei arrived at the dacha after his return from England, his mother and Babushka had already bottled some strawberries and raspberries. It was a yearly ritual that Andrei knew so well, when they were all caught up in a storm of activity to make sure that they had enough food to get through the winter and early spring. A little later, the September weekends were spent gathering mushrooms in the woods, and preparing them for drying. This was the way to get vitamins and fresh vegetables and fruit in the six barren months.

The dacha was Andrei's favourite place in the world, just like Woody Bay for Margaret. He did not need much company but had a friend called Ilya who lived at a neighbouring dacha, much bigger and better built, with a massive porcelain stove in its high-ceilinged living-room, so that the house could be used in the winter. One year Andrei had come with Ilya in January and they had gone skiing through the woods and across the stream to visit Andrei's own dacha, looking very small, but cosy and protected beneath a deep covering of fresh snow. Andrei skied back across the stream from which they drew their crystal clear drinking water in the summer, happy that his family's dacha was safe.

In late June, not long before Andrei had gone to England, he and his family spent a day at the dacha. Something happened that had helped prepare Andrei for his visit there. It was to change his life for ever.

Igor had invited his old professor and tutor from his university years in Leningrad to visit them. The professor was a member of the Academy of Sciences, an 'Academician', the highest honour the Soviet state could award to a scholar. 'Akademik Dmitry', Igor called him, out of affection as well as respect.

The Academician arrived on the first train of the day and went back to Moscow on the last. He spent quite a lot of time talking with Andrei, in English as well as Russian. He asked Andrei about the English books he read at school and listened to him as he told him about what he was learning of Russian history at school.

'There is more to it than that,' he said quietly as Andrei told him how his text book told the story of exploitation and serfdom in the years before the Communist revolution of 1917.

And, carefully, he narrated the earliest years of Russia's history. It was like a poem, both epic and lyric, the way the Academician told the story: that Russia, then called *Rus*, was created by a mixture of Slav tribes from near the Black Sea and migrant Varangians coming south from Scandinavia; that she flourished at Kiev in Ukraine; and that the centre of the Russian people moved north east when Moscow was founded in 1147. He said nothing about politics or recent history, but seemed to have boundless confidence that something of the old Russia, *Rus*, survived and would one day be reborn. The Academician was speaking to Andrei, but Igor and Natalya were half-listening as they prepared a special meal at the table.

'If only the Academician would write a book about our history for school children,' Natalya said quietly.

'They would not publish it,' said Igor. 'He loves old *Rus* too much for them.'

'He tells the story of our country so clearly and briefly, but it's all there.' Natalya's tone was wistful.

'He always used to say 'brevity is the sign of good manners and courtesy in a scholar' when he was lecturing to us. Do you remember?'

The two of them laughed at the memory of the days when the Academician inspired them to become scholars in Leningrad, still devastated by the effects of Hitler's blockade of the city.

The Academician gestured and pointed out through the door.

'I see *Rus*, there,' he said to Andrei. Andrei looked at the silver birch trees, green and young, a mass of lilac and wild flowers and above them a boundless sky.

From that day Andrei called the dacha *Rus* and the word caught on with all the family, especially with Babushka. She had sat in the corner, listening and preparing vegetables, as the Academician had his talk with Andrei. They were the same age. Her face, like his, was heavily lined. Her eyes, and his, shone as he spoke of the birth of Russia a thousand years ago, and of his hopes. Andrei had a feeling that the Academician and Babushka already knew each other, but no one said anything about that.

Something new and strange entered Andrei's mind and soul. He would tell no one about it for now, but never again would he fully trust what the Communist leaders of their country said. The Academician's words and his grandmother's shining face told him some truth which the world in which he lived did its best to hide or destroy. He felt that they had within them something that he wanted for himself.

Igor and Andrei moved the table out of the dacha. They set it among the lilac and silver birch trees. Natalya cut lilac blossom and put it in a vase. Andrei hurried to the stream to get water for them to drink. Natalya was cooking a chicken. During the summer Babushka lived at the dacha for four months, and each year she kept a few chickens which a neighbour let her have. To use a young chicken for a meal was a rare treat; usually they provided eggs until they reached a great age and were just gristle and bone, fit only for making soup.

Babushka and the Academician sat talking on their own. Both of them had been born in St Petersburg at the turn of the century, well before it was renamed Petrograd in the First World War and Leningrad after Lenin's death in 1924.

Babushka and the Academician had been in Leningrad throughout the nine hundred days of the blockade.

'They were hard times in the War, but we were united, strong against the Nazis although we were starving,' Babushka said.

'Hard, Ludmila Ivanovna, but it was harder before that and afterwards,' said the Academician. 'In the 1930s, remember, "Only the dead could smile".'

He was quoting Leningrad's greatest poetess who wrote those words during Stalin's Great Terror. She was one of its chroniclers and one of its victims. She had lost her family to it and had been an outcast because of her religious faith and her honesty. The poem which the Academician quoted had been passed by word of mouth.

Babushka looked startled. Even now, three years after the death of Stalin, the habit of silence about the sufferings before and after the War was powerful.

The family and their guest sat down at the table in the warm afternoon sun. They ate pickled herring and sour cream, and then with the chicken there were potatoes from last year's crop and a bottle of Mukuzani wine from Georgia in the Caucasus mountains, more than a thousand miles to the south. The Academician had brought this back with him from Tbilisi, the capital of Georgia, when he had visited it for a conference. Then, there was one of the last bottles of last year's raspberries, and tea from the samovar.

There was something about the Academician's expression and quiet manner and about his conversation with Andrei that reassured Babushka. After the meal they began to talk on their own about their earliest days in St Petersburg; the snow on the Nevsky Prospekt at Christmas as shoppers, some of them in sleighs, hurried up and down the wide, elegant avenue with its bright shops; the glorious, mysterious services in the cathedrals and churches; the celebrations at Easter; the 'White Nights' of late June and July when the atmosphere was joyful and the daylight unending; and the sudden short autumn and the onset of winter when there was so little sun.

In Moscow Babushka rarely met people of her own age who had lived through all the joys and sorrows of St Petersburg. In the summer months every year she lived like a farmer's wife, a peasant, but in her youth she had attended a good school and she loved Russian literature. She knew English as well as French.

On and on they talked, just the two of them in a world no one else was old enough to share.

The sun was setting.

Soon Igor would take the Academician to the local station to catch the electric train back to Moscow. Out of sight of Igor and Natalya the Academician said goodbye to Babushka. Reverently he made the sign of the Cross over her in the Russian Orthodox way, and Babushka responded in the same style. Their talk had shown them that they shared something deeper than their years of deprivation, something which those years had made even stronger.

Andrei came into the room quietly as, each in turn, they made the sign of the Cross.

'Remember *Rus*, Andrei,' said the Academician, seriously but with a smile. 'Your Babushka will tell you more about it. She will give you the feel for it.'

And he was gone.

'He was baptised, wasn't he, Babushka?' Andrei asked.

'Of course, Andrei, we all were in those days,' she replied.

Babushka had come to Moscow to live with Igor and Natalya immediately after the Second World War. She had lost all her other relatives in Leningrad before or during the War. Stalin had not yet again struck down the Church which for his own ends he had freed a little from persecution for a few years. He had done that, just to raise the Russian people's morale. In his heart he knew that they would fight for Holy Russia and her Christian faith, but not for him and the Communist Party. Soon he would again torment all Christian believers and try to extinguish the Church's life, but that was a year or so away. Between them, Lenin, Trotsky and Stalin inflicted the severest persecution on the church that it had suffered in two thousand years.

For a month or two in 1945, after the Red Army's victory, Stalin seemed despite himself pensive, almost in awe of the endurance of the Russian people. It was a rare lapse. Stalin's greatest skill was his self-control, his ability to keep silent while he made his plans to destroy each of his rivals in turn, keeping the rest guessing, encouraging them in the vain hope that he would spare them, and using them against each victim until their turn came to be killed.

In 1946 Babushka took Andrei and had him baptised by a priest in Moscow. She gave the priest a false surname. She knew that the secret police would ask him for details of the children he christened, and she did not want to threaten Andrei's future or Igor's employment.

When she was alone with Andrei, Babushka

sometimes told him the story of this secret baptism, and Andrei knew from his earliest childhood not to talk about this with anyone, even his parents. He was not sure whether they knew about it and he never mentioned it to them.

There were so many things it was safer not to talk about, so many questions that could not be asked. How was it that he had been chosen to go to England that summer when Ilya, with a powerful family and a grand dacha, had to be content with a holiday in the Crimea, swimming in the Black Sea, safely in the Soviet Union?

Andrei did not ask. He wondered whether it had happened because of his father's friendship with the Academician. His conversation with him about *Rus* and the way he and Babushka had talked together gave him the feeling that the Academician was somehow watching over him, like a godfather. That sense would always comfort him.

For two and a half weeks at the dacha, after his return from England, Andrei spent his time with Ilya. They swam in the lake and explored the forest. On the last day of August they returned to Moscow. The following day term began, and they took their places in their new class.

Sussex

TERM started at Mr Durham's school. Margaret began to get used to the new routine there. It was a wet and dismal autumn.

Arguments about Suez continued in Parliament and the press, but it was events in Hungary that worried Margaret and her parents. Through September and October they followed what was happening there as closely as they could. John picked up broadcasts from Budapest on his short-wave radio. He was amazed by the boldness of the Hungarian leaders, calling for free elections and a neutral status for their country, like that of Austria.

The Hungarian Communist Party appointed a new Prime Minister, Imre Nagy. Nagy had been dismissed by the Communists not long before. Now he seemed to be the right man to lead the reforms. Many Hungarians were calling for the end of the Communist state and the creation of a democracy with several political parties.

Helena wrote to the Durhams to thank them for their friendship and kindness and for the week at

Woody Bay. She told them that Tibor had been visiting friends all over Hungary. John guessed that he must be working with the freedom movement in some way, producing leaflets or taking part in meetings. After that letter there was no more news.

At half-term, in late October, there were some out-breaks of violence in Hungary, but the situation seemed to be generally peaceful. The Soviet Army of occupation was even reported to have withdrawn. There was a hope in the West that the Soviet Union had accepted the changes demanded by the popula-tion and that it could all happen without the fear that Soviet security was at risk. There were four days of calm.

On Sunday night, the fourth of November, every-thing changed. The Soviet Union launched an air-raid on Budapest. Some parts of the city which had barely recovered from the battles there at the end of the Second World War were again engulfed in flames and explosions.

On Monday afternoon when Margaret was eating her tea at home in Sussex, the television announced that there would be a programme that evening with a film of recent events in Hungary. Television was still a novelty for the Durhams. They had recently bought their set, a bulky cube covered in thin mahogany veneer, standing on a table in the corner of the room.

'They could be dead,' Margaret thought. 'Tibor and Helena could be dead. How could Andrei's country do this to their allies?'

It was bonfire night, always a great event in Sussex. Fireworks were blazing and exploding in the gardens all around them. It seemed a pale image of the explosions and firepower in Hungary.

At a quarter to nine all the family sat in front of the television set. The programme titles on the screen declared 'Panorama, your window on the world'; a black and white picture, with a lot of white snow flickering over the screen. The usual introductory music was played. It was a tinny sound.

There was a brief item about Suez. The presenter showed on various maps the positions taken by British and French troops, and explained how an international force would take over from them following the armistice. It was clear that, because of hostility around the world to what Britain, France and Israel had done in Egypt, all the British troops would soon be returning to Britain. The whole operation had collapsed, leaving a sense of shame and humiliation.

'Sir Anthony Eden won't be Prime Minister for long,' said John.

The programme moved on to the crisis in Hungary. The reporter was a thin young man with a mass of wild hair. He said that his film had been taken the previous week in Hungary. He had visited the country with a Hungarian interpreter. At that time, he explained, it had seemed that the Hungarian uprising was succeeding; that the Soviet Union had agreed to withdraw its troops; and that Hungary would become a representative democracy with free elections and free speech. All that had changed because on Sunday night Soviet planes bombed Budapest and the Soviet Army took up dominant positions everywhere.

'This film is still worth showing,' he added, 'because it shows how widespread was the support to change the system, to introduce democracy in Hungary. It makes it obvious that if the Communist system survives, it can do so only through the overwhelming force of the Soviet Union and the same may well apply to the other countries of Eastern Europe.'

In the film the reporter was shown travelling through southern Hungary towards Budapest. Groups of people were holding up banners in support of freedom for Hungary, people of all ages, men, women and many children, even young ones, younger than Margaret.

'Look at them,' said Margaret. 'They are like the juniors at the primary school, with their teacher.'

The people in the pictures seemed to have a sense of purpose and unity and to be elated at the possibility of change.

The scene moved to a town called Magyarouar. The mood there was much darker. Blood-stains were shown on the ground in the town square.

'This is the scene of a massacre,' said the reporter. 'Up to a hundred people died here during a peaceful protest. A large crowd gathered last Monday in front of the local headquarters of the secret police. After some quiet discussion between the protesters and the commander of the secret police, he gave the order to open fire. We were told by the local people, all still in a state of stunned shock, that about a hundred people were killed. But despite this horror, or because of it, the reforms are continuing. On the same day as this slaughter occurred, the new government of Imre Nagy declared the end of one party, Communist rule, proclaimed a ceasefire and the Soviet forces began to withdraw.'

'They just withdrew to gather their forces in greater strength,' said John.

'No wonder Tibor and Helena were so tense a lot of the time,' replied Margaret, 'And Andrei...'

Fresh scenes came up on the screen, nearer Budapest. A group of young people was marching towards the camera, singing, exultant and happy.

'Tibor!' said Margaret.

'Tibor!' said the others.

'It can't be, but it is...'

'He looks different, much happier.'

'Yes, full of life. Here he always seemed to be on a leash, chained up.'

'He looks free,' said Margaret. 'He likes the danger... But where's Helena?'

There was no sign of her, and after a few seconds the film moved on to Budapest itself.

The reporter reappeared in the studio. Again he explained that everything had changed for the worse since his film had been taken. By now people were dying in Hungary in resistance to the Soviet invasion. The withdrawal seven days earlier had been nothing but pretence.

Hungary enjoyed only four days' freedom. One or two radio stations continued to broadcast for a day or two after that. They appealed to the West to intervene to save them.

There was no chance of that. Hungary was doomed to continue as a Communist satellite of the Soviet Union for thirty three more years. The West was too preoccupied with Suez and the Presidential election campaign in the United States. President Eisenhower won by a landslide.

In Egypt, Colonel Nasser had already been adopting a pro-Soviet policy. Russia had always wanted to weaken the power of the British Empire in the Indian Ocean and beyond and so create instability and open the way for Communist *coups d'etat*. It was all part of Khrushchev's plan for spreading Soviet power. Robbing Great Britain of security at the Suez Canal was part of his grand design. Nasser was positioning Egypt as a crucial Soviet ally, which it remained for over twenty years.

The 'Panorama' programme ended.

'But what about Tibor and Helena and their family?' asked Margaret. 'What will happen to Tibor if he is caught by the Russians? What can Andrei think about it all?'

Russia

IN Moscow, many hundreds of miles to the East, after tossing and turning in bed for hours, Andrei was deeply asleep.

That afternoon like Margaret, he had been watching television after school, at Ilya's flat. Ilya's mother, Vera, had been at school with Natalya in Leningrad and from time to time she arranged for Andrei to come to spend some time with him. Ilya did not have many friends because of his father's position.

In a cavernous, echoing room with high ceilings, sitting on heavy wooden chairs, Andrei and Ilya saw newsreel pictures and heard a story utterly at odds with what the Durhams were to see a little later that day.

There was a report about the international outrage that had followed the action that Great Britain and France had taken in the Suez Canal.

'Even the Americans have opposed this act of war,' said the announcer. 'The Soviet Union and our allies have taken steps at the United Nations Organisation in New York to bring the hostilities to an end and to force Great Britain, France and Israel to withdraw from the Canal Zone and make way for an inter-national peace-keeping force.'

Then the announcer reported on events in Hungary.

'A counter-revolutionary force has tried to seize power in Hungary. Imperialists and capitalists from America and Western Europe are trying to reassert themselves there. Their aim is to deprive the Hun-garian people of all the gains achieved by socialism since 1945 and to break the ties of friendship which bind Hungary, the Soviet Union and our other allies in Eastern Europe in the Warsaw Pact. For that reason the government of the Hungarian Democratic Republic has called on the Soviet Union and our allies for fraternal assistance. They have received speedy help.'

The news bulletin was followed by a short film of tanks gathering to enter Hungary and of aircraft taking off on their mission. There was no mention of Hungarian casualties or of the popular uprising.

Andrei and Ilya did not talk about the news. They never did, nor did their parents in front of them.

'What would Akademik Dmitry say?' Andrei thought to himself.

Turning away from the television, Andrei and Ilya ate their tea and did their homework. They both attended a special school where almost all the lessons were taught in English. But for that, their mothers would never have met again. At the end of the War Vera had married a man much older than her, high up in the Communist party, and she and Natalya immediately lost contact. Andrei and Ilya met at school. Otherwise, Andrei would never have visited this block of flats which was reserved for important government officials.

Andrei had won his place at the school against fierce competition two years ago. His scholarship was one of a tiny number available to children of people who were not members of the Communist elite.

Ilya put out the ivory chess pieces on a little ebony and birch-wood table. Each of the boys won a game. They were well matched.

Ilya's father had not returned from his office by the time Andrei left. It would be ten o'clock before his chauffeur drove him home in his long black car with its thick curtains drawn across the windows in the back to prevent prying eyes from seeing people like him.

Andrei had a cup of tea with his parents and Babushka before going to bed. He said goodnight to them and went into his bedroom, a small box-room with books piled to the ceiling.

Before he got ready for bed he went to the chest of drawers at the foot of his bed. The chest was the only piece of Babushka's furniture that had survived the fires and bombs of the blockade of Leningrad. It was elegant, made well before 1917, and somehow it had been spared the furnace even in the third winter of the War when so much had to be burnt to produce a little warmth. Babushka had given the chest to Andrei. In its bottom drawer Andrei kept his special treasures. It was the rarest of those that he was looking for now.

Eleven years earlier, Igor, Andrei's father, had been twenty-two years old. He had served in the Soviet Army on the front line as Stalin's forces pushed their way across Eastern Europe, pursuing the Nazis who fought them fiercely all the way. Through Poland, south into Czechoslovakia and Hungary, west into Germany, suffering immense casualties but exacting from their enemies and the civilian population a terrible price for the invasion of Russia, the huge Army rolled on.

Soviet soldiers raised the hammer and sickle flag above the Reichstag in Berlin. Others pressed on to the River Elbe where they finally met the Western Allies. Soviet, British and American soldiers greeted each other warmly and celebrated for several days until Stalin ordered that such 'fraternisation' should stop. It was a hint of what was to come.

The Soviet generals had driven their Army as fast as possible to the West to reduce the power of the Americans and British and to assert Stalin's claims in Europe. At one time Stalin had hoped to reach much further, but that objective eluded him.

Igor somehow survived. Only about three in a hundred of his age-group in the Red Army did so. He was lucky. In his body he was not seriously wounded, but for years his mind remained crippled by what he had seen and had to do in battle.

Igor's uncle, his father's brother, Oleg, was a diplomat. At the end of the war he was working in the Soviet Ministry of Foreign Affairs, liaising with the British Embassy. He was involved in producing a special newspaper, in Russian, which Stalin had, reluctantly, let the British produce and distribute. 'Britanskiy Soyuznik' it was called, 'The British Ally'. Stalin allowed the paper to be published as some sort of acknowledgement of all that Great Britain did for the Soviet Union from the moment of Hitler's attack in June 1941. The British sent weapons, tanks, food and other supplies to help Stalin resist the invaders.

So *Britanskiy Soyuznik* began its short life, produced in the British Embassy and giving news of the War and the British point of view. Stalin ordered that its distribution should be tightly controlled. He always did all he could to stop his people hearing any point of view other than his own. As soon as he could, he had the paper closed down but in those few years it had a surprising impact on those who read it.

When Igor returned from the army in 1945, he read through the old copies that Uncle Oleg had stored. It was this that helped him to recover, he always thought. The news in the *British Ally* was the story of the events through which he had lived but it was told in a way that gave some hope for the future. Truth has a strange power.

Andrei was looking for a copy of *Britanskiy Soyuznik* with a photograph that fascinated him. It was of the three war leaders, taken when they met at Yalta in the Crimea in February 1945.

Stalin sat to the left of the others, smiling, impassive and cunning. Churchill had offered him British support within hours of hearing of Hitler's invasion.

He said to one of his secretaries on that day that he would speak up 'for the Devil himself' if he were fighting Hitler. It was meant as a joke, but in his heart Churchill must have known that he was creating a diabolical alliance. Why else would he have used those words? The tragedy was that there was no alternative.

All the spring and summer of 1941 Churchill had been warning Stalin that Hitler was planning to attack him. Stalin did not believe him. Stalin did not trust Churchill, who had worked hard in 1917 and the years that followed to oppose the Bolsheviks. Besides that, Churchill had no idea that Stalin himself had for years been taking all the steps needed to launch a surprise attack on Hitler as soon as he could, but Hitler got wind of Stalin's plans and launched his attack, 'Operation Barbarossa', too soon for Stalin.

To attack Russia and open a war on two fronts was suicide for Germany. In *Mein Kampf* Hitler had written as much in the mid 1920s. In 1941 he did not even equip his army with proper winter clothing or supplies or make sure that he had enough of the right fuel for his tanks and transport for the Russian winter. Stalin's agents in Germany told him this. That was why he did not believe that Hitler would attack him. Being sane, cold and hard-headed himself, Stalin did not grasp that Hitler was demented and hot-blooded. He thought that, when he warned him of the coming attack, Churchill was just trying to cause trouble between him and Hitler too soon, before his troops could move west to attack Germany. Stalin could not risk doing anything that might put at risk his own attack on Germany, at a time that suited him.

Next to Stalin in the Yalta photograph, in the centre sat President Roosevelt, the leader of a nation not ravaged by war, immensely powerful, in fact strengthened by the conflict, with all its industry working, no unemployment, no food shortages, and no rationing. Roosevelt was leaning towards Stalin, as if ingratiating himself to him, almost excluding the third leader, Churchill.

To the right of Roosevelt sat Churchill, the oldest of the three, in his seventieth year. As Prime Minister he had endured the burden of the war longest, fourteen months longer than Stalin (who had been Hitler's secret ally until June 1941) and eighteen months longer than Roosevelt. Even when Japan had attacked, without warning, the American fleet at Pearl Harbour, it had been Hitler who had first taken the step of declaring war on the Americans.

'*Britanskiy Soyuznik*' told how the leaders had met at Yalta to prepare for the peace in Europe after they had defeated Hitler. But whatever Churchill's hopes or Roosevelt's delusions or Stalin's malice, the peace had become a 'Cold War', an ice age, with Europe and the World divided by the Iron Curtain.

'What is happening in Hungary will make it colder still,' Andrei thought.

He pictured Margaret and her parents, and Tibor and Helena. He lived yet again the memories of their time at Woody Bay. For all he knew, it was now politically dangerous to keep the photograph of the three leaders sitting together as allies. He thought of his hopes of meeting his new friends again, hugging his knees up to his chest under the blankets.

'No, not "for ever and ever",' he thought. 'Never again... Never again...'

Andrei tossed and turned in bed, and for hours he could not sleep.

Hungary

TIBOR had not slept for forty-eight hours.

All the time he had been on the move, from house to house and flat to flat. Soviet planes screamed in low over Budapest and tanks took up their positions. Tibor and his friends were given weapons by Hungarian soldiers who had come over to their side. They filled bottles with petrol to hurl at the tanks as they rolled into the city. They listened to the free radio station giving them news of the invasion and heard urgent appeals to the West to intervene to save Hungary.

By midnight on Monday Tibor was holed up in a flat at the top of a block overlooking one of the main roads leading into Budapest. The Soviet Army was advancing steadily along the road. Tanks fired their cannon and the walls and windows of the flat shook. Gradually the Hungarians were pushed back, withdrawing street by street, harassing the tanks and destroying some of them but overwhelmed by their number and power.

'Now, Tibor, now!' shouted the commander of his group. 'Get out of here *now!*'

Tibor did not hear him above the fighting. He was left alone, looking out of the window of the fifth floor flat. He did not notice that his companions had left until it was too late for him to escape with them, scurrying away in a side street.

The tanks rattled on. Infantry soldiers moved along the avenue behind them shocked and frightened by the fierce resistance. They had expected nothing like this. They had been told that they were going to help the Hungarian people, their allies who were crying out for their support against a foreign counter-revolutionary movement. Systematically, the soldiers entered every building, nervously searching for snipers, eager to kill rather than be killed.

White flags flew from the windows of many flats.

Tibor did not fly a white flag. It was the flag of Free Hungary that he tied to his rifle, with the Soviet hammer and sickle cut out of it.

A Russian soldier found him like that, his rifle held across his chest. The soldier was not much older than Tibor. He did not want to be there, or even in the Army. He did not know why this huge force had been sent to Budapest only ten years after his father had fought his way here across Eastern Europe, simply to free Hungary from the Nazis as he had believed. The young soldier wanted only to get it over with and get home. He kicked open the door and fired.

Tibor slept at last.

In their flat on the other side of the city, Eva, Tibor's mother, was stuffing a few belongings into two old haversacks.

'Bread... sausage,' she said to herself. She added a few apples, two pullovers, underwear and a few pairs of socks. There was room for nothing more. Giori and Helena had to be able to carry them and, perhaps, walk the best part of a hundred miles.

Eva was determined that they should escape. She had lived in Budapest before the Second World War, and through it, and for ten years since then.

'Liberation...' she said with contempt. '*Liberation!*' She spat the word out.

In the late 1930s Eva had seen her government appease Hitler, yet suffer invasion by the Nazis and then be 'liberated' in the words of Communist propaganda but in fact enslaved by the Soviet Army. She lost her husband in the fighting. And the years of control and terror at the hands of the Soviet Union were as bad as the years of war; even worse, as they lasted twice as long.

She had seen her cousin lose his work on some false political charge; then he was sent to prison where he had died. She had not seen his body, and no one had been allowed by the police to attend the funeral, if there had been one.

Eva had worked as an English teacher and earned money for her children. Above all, she had concealed her opinions: from the secret police, from her employers, from her trade union (which was state-controlled), from her children. She worked hard and she had been trusted by the authorities. Only in this way had Tibor and Helena been given the opportunity by her trade union to go on the exchange trip to England.

But her efforts had all been in vain. Despite her silence and self-control for so long, Tibor was infected by the spirit which spread among Hungarians, especially the young people, that summer. Perhaps the visit to England had increased his free spirit, although he had not said much about his time there. It had been Helena who had done all the talking, and that had been about the sea, her new friends, including Andrei the Russian boy: nothing political or dangerous at all.

Now she had to send Giori and Helena on alone.

'Unless you go now, it may be too late.'

'But what about you?' said Giori.

'And Tibor?' said Helena.

'I'll find Tibor and come on to catch you up. We'll meet at the frontier.'

'You'll never find him on your own.' Giori glanced at her and saw her determined expression, and fell silent.

'We'll help you, Mother,' said Helena. 'We know his friends better than you do. You'll need us to help find him.'

But Eva insisted, so now she was stuffing the few essentials into the haversacks. And Giori was walking round the flat, looking at the old furniture that belonged to his grandfather. He knew that he would never see it again, that from now his life would be different, if he had one at all.

Giori was a matter of fact boy. He would never feel like this again. He was not a romantic like Helena, or a revolutionary like Tibor. Eva had often joked with her husband that Giori was the only real Hungarian child they had: practical and steady, he would always cope, feeling at home whatever the circumstances.

But now something was turning deep inside Giori. He could not express it and would not have done so if he had been able. But he knew that something was ending. He knew he would never see his mother again, and he knew that he must not say this to her or to Helena. He knew that this was his mother's will, and he was closer to her than the others were, for she too was his sort of Hungarian. 'Do not dramatise anything; live on through these circumstances; whatever else you do, just endure.'

But in those few minutes Giori went around the flat and took everything into his mind and stored it there. He would never speak of it, never share it with others. People would say, 'Amazing how cool Giori is, how he copes... Nothing can touch Giori.' And they would be wrong, but they would never know.

So Eva and Giori were dry-eyed as she almost pushed him and Helena out of the front door, down the stairs and into the street. She helped them up a ladder into an old lorry which a teacher from their school had obtained.

The lorry was crowded, overflowing with children and young people. They were Hungary's future and they were trying to escape. The country's future would now be half at home and half abroad because, although Hungary was a small country, not everyone could escape.

Eva embraced her colleague, Dodi. He was in his fifties. He had fought the Nazis in the Second World War and was later trusted by the Communist authorities. His family was all dead. And now he was trying to escape. If anyone could do so, he would get his lorry with the children to the border with Austria. For that was the only safe way to go, towards the west. To the north was Czechoslovakia, held firmly by the Soviet Army; to the south was Yugoslavia, controlled by its own Communist government; to the east was the Soviet Union itself, and Rumania, under another brutal Communist tyranny.

Giori held Helena firmly around the shoulders. She sobbed and called out, 'Come quickly, Mother. We'll wait for you both at the border.'

'We'll get there before you, I expect,' said Eva. 'Tibor will have to make it up to us for what he's put us through.'

The sound of the tanks in the distance cut short their farewells. Dodi started the engine and the lorry set off down the street in clouds of black fumes.

It was a race against time. Dodi's lorry joined a trickle of vehicles and people, all moving west. As he turned onto the wide avenue the trickle became a steady stream, making for the border with Austria before the Soviet forces could take control of the Hungarian guards there and force them to close the escape route.

Eva went back to her flat.

A mile or two separated her from Tibor on the other side of the city. It was as difficult for her to know what had happened to him as it was for the Durhams in Sussex.

Eva knew as well as Giori that she would never see him and Helena again, but she could not abandon Tibor, so like her husband when he was young.

'*Liberation!*' She spat it out again. 'At least Giori and Helena will have a chance to be really free.'

Tibor had been named after Eva's husband, and he was like him in every way. That was how she remembered Big Tibor. When she first met him in his last years at school he was raging against the appeasement of Hitler by Hungary's authoritarian government; and then fighting against the Nazis when they invaded, but not trusting the Soviet allies as they began to take over his country in 1945. Little Tibor, five years old when his father died, had carried on his true spirit, and still did.

'There is a price to pay for that free spirit,' Eva thought. 'We are both bound to pay it.'

Eva had a great faith in Giori.

'Giori will make sure that Helena escapes, and then she will be able to cope... She will take care of Giori and he will take care of her,' Eva said to herself as she went over to the old oak chest in the corner of her bedroom.

She opened the bottom drawer.

'It must still be here, unless Tibor...'

But Tibor had not discovered her secret. At the back of the drawer, wrapped carefully in the remains of an old red silk dress, in which she had danced with Big Tibor a lifetime ago, was the revolver that he had used in the War.

'How the Communists would have punished us if they had found it,' she thought, as she unwrapped the gun. But her quiet, conformist life had given rise to no suspicion.

The night was cold. Eva put on warm clothes although nothing could really protect her from what she was now facing. She hid the gun inside her coat and locked the flat.

As the sky lightened she set off in the direction of the fighting which seemed to be drawing nearer. Despite the dawn, the blaze of cannon fire from the tanks became brighter; the explosions grew louder.

Eva was moving against the tide. There were elderly men and women, dressed soberly and carrying suitcases; young mothers with children in prams piled high with their luggage. All of them were escaping from the centre of the storm, while she was forcing her way into it.

Eva met a few young men, hardly older than Tibor, running past her, holding weapons, Molotov cocktails and revolvers; and among them a girl, Monika, Tibor's girlfriend; not really his girlfriend, he was too shy, too intense. Eva was shocked to see her here, armed with bottles of petrol to throw at Soviet tanks, and even more troubled that Tibor was not with her. He would have stayed with her if he had been able, to protect her. They would have fought shoulder to shoulder.

'Aunt Eva,' Monika called out. She was not really Eva's niece but was treated as one of the family.

'Aunt Eva, you must go back. The tanks are crushing us, only a few hundred metres away.'

'Tibor?' said Eva.

'We lost him... It was in a block of flats. We had to fall back. We got separated... We didn't see that he was missing. He wouldn't leave, Aunt Eva, he wouldn't pull back with us. I am so sorry. Forgive me, Aunt Eva...'

Eva turned off the main avenue into the side streets: smoke, the stench of gunfire, and a few buildings half-ablaze.

She pressed on. Now she was behind the line of tanks pushing, roaring along the avenue. She ran back to the main road, trying to hide, scurrying from door to door. The Russian soldiers were entering each building as they came to it, shooting, bringing out prisoners, snipers who had tried to stop their advance.

Eva gazed at them, hoping against hope to see Tibor. Since Big Tibor's death he had been the centre of her life. Without him, there was nothing, no hope, no meaning, no purpose for her.

She crouched in a doorway. A sniper's bullet aimed at the Soviet soldiers caught her in the neck, and she died in the entrance of the building where Tibor himself had been shot dead earlier that night, but not knowing that she was so near him.

Dodi drove his lorry carefully but as fast as he could through the dawn, through the morning. Some of the youngest children sang, and their parents encouraged them. For them it was like an unexpected day off school in the late Indian summer.

Sweat dripped down Dodi's face. The engine roared and groaned. The driving cab was stifling. Dodi was also consumed by fear for his passengers; not for himself. He planned to drive the lorry back to Budapest and bring out more who wanted to flee the Soviet troops.

The needle of the fuel gauge moved in jerks towards empty. Dodi had no idea how much was left in the tank.

'Let me borrow that fishing rod,' he asked a little boy who for some reason had brought his toy rod with him. 'I'll bring it back safe to you.'

The boy's mother gently took the rod and gave it to Dodi. Her husband had given their son the rod for his sixth birthday the week before, but he had stayed behind in Budapest to face the tanks.

Dodi opened the cap on the fuel tank and inserted the rod. Withdrawing it he found that only a few inches of fuel were left. Whether they would find a petrol station in time, he had no idea. He wiped the rod and returned it to the little boy who proudly held onto it.

'When will Daddy come?' he kept asking his mother. 'Can we all go fishing together when we get to Vienna?'

They drove into a village festooned with the flags of Free Hungary. The flag flew even on the police station.

Dodi knew he was taking a risk but he had no alternative. He pulled the lorry over into the yard. There was a fuel pump there for the police vehicles, guarded by a policeman. The policeman looked at the passengers in Dodi's lorry. After hesitating for a moment he nodded to him. Dodi got out and opened the tank.

'That's all I can give you,' said the policeman after a while. 'It should get you most of the way.'

The children waved to the policeman, and he waved back. The engine roared into life. Dodi pulled the lorry out to rejoin the traffic heading west.

The journey got slower. There were all manner of ancient vehicles on the road. Dodi picked up a few families whose cars had broken down, and the lorry was as full as he dared. They passed men and women harvesting potatoes in the fields. They saw market stalls piled high with tomatoes, peppers (green, red, and yellow), enormous peaches and apples, the produce of the richest soil in Europe over which so many battles had been fought down the centuries. It was soil created to give a peaceful, contented life to a settled population, but such a life had hardly ever been known there. There would be just a few decades of peace and then another upheaval, another invasion. That was the pattern there, and whether it would ever change, who could tell?

Giori was determined that Helena and he should know that sort of peaceful, settled life, however far they had to travel to find it. He was very quiet and kept his arm around Helena, holding her and their haversacks tightly. He was hoping that Mother and Tibor would join them, but he was working out what they would do if they did not.

Dodi drove on towards the frontier. They passed the most fertile region of all, hundreds of thousands of acres stretching out within an enormous bend of the River Danube. The valley was dense with trees, their leaves now falling, golden, yellow and red, and at intervals within the forest there were some big houses which looked desolate. Giori knew that they belonged to the Communist elite. Some of them had supported the uprising against the Soviet control of the country. What the others were doing, Giori dreaded to think. Perhaps some of them had fled to Russia or Czechoslovakia, to support the invading forces now retaking Budapest. It would not be long before they could again enjoy their country houses.

They were ten miles from the frontier with Austria, only forty miles from Vienna. Dodi's lorry lost power and stopped. He drew it onto the roadside and tried to start the engine, but there was no life in it. Again, he borrowed the little boy's fishing rod, but this time it showed no fuel at all. All the passengers got off and began to walk to the frontier. Dodi joined them; he hoped that he would be able to get back to his lorry with fuel to make the return journey.

Giori and Helena walked on, not looking back, surrounded by the other passengers, all soon to be refugees. A few yards away from them, on either side of the road, were fields in which workers were labouring in perfect peace.

The people heading west were caught up in turmoil, rushing to escape, but it was difficult to believe that there was anything to escape from. It would have been easy to believe that Mother and Tibor were safely in their flat, waiting for them to return. But Giori and Helena pressed on. As darkness closed in they reached the frontier, the Iron Curtain between East and West.

And it was so easy to cross: no formalities, no difficulties, for the world was watching this frontier. Soon there would be television cameras here, sending their pictures to homes in Western Europe and America. In England, Margaret would see the pictures next Sunday afternoon but she would not see Helena with whom she had spent two weeks only three months ago, or Giori about whom Helena and Tibor had told her, for Giori and Helena were crossing the border at the very beginning of the exodus before the cameras were in position.

Just before they went across, to be enveloped in the care of the Red Cross, Giori suddenly stopped. He knelt down at the roadside and took out his handkerchief. With both hands he slowly scraped up some earth and tiny pebbles and put it all in the handkerchief and tied a knot. All this he did without emotion, but he avoided Helena's eye. He took it to her. Helena embraced Giori for a long time. Together, they carefully put the little packet of Hungarian soil into Helena's haversack. Then, arm in arm, they walked across to the West, through a tear in the Curtain that would soon be closed.

1956-1961
Hungary and Sussex

IN the Red Cross camp in Austria just across the border from Hungary, Helena and Giori waited for several days, always hoping to see Mother and Tibor arrive. A week and more passed. There was no news. The border was closed. The security guards on the Hungarian side, by now under Russian orders, became much more severe.

In the end Helena decided to telephone the Durhams. There was no one else to turn to.

'You must come to us,' said John.

He spoke to Giori in Hungarian as well as to Helena, for a couple of minutes.

'You must come to us,' he told him. 'There is a home for both of you here. Margaret won't be lonely now.'

With the help of the Red Cross Giori and Helena set off across Western Europe to England.

'We saw Tibor on the television,' John told them a few days later when they got off the ferry at Folkestone harbour. 'Just for a moment. He flashed across the screen, full of fire and determination.'

'There were many like him,' said Giori. 'Many died like him.'

'That was when we decided,' said Margaret. 'If you needed us, we wanted you to come here.'

'We thank you,' said Giori to John and Barbara. 'My sister and I thank you for your welcome.'

He spoke formally, his cheeks pink with embarrassment.

'We are lucky,' he said. 'We know it.'

'No, we *want* you,' said John and Barbara.

'For ever and ever,' said Margaret.

She and Helena laughed, and explained why, to Giori. For just a moment they spoke of Andrei.

In temporary offices government officials interviewed the refugees. Giori and Helena were dealt with quickly, and given permission to go and live with the Durhams.

The new family of five passed easily through all the controls, past the Immigration and Customs staff, past the members of the Women's Voluntary Services organising sandwiches to eat and tea to drink, past railwaymen sorting out the trains.

Together the five of them started the journey home to Battle.

Most of the Hungarian refugees had nowhere to go. The British government opened several old army camps for them as temporary accommodation. Soon most of them would move on, into private housing and jobs. There was a warm welcome for them. A public collection raised two million pounds in a few weeks, a huge amount of money in those days.

Many of the refugees went on to play an outstanding part in the life of Great Britain. Fifty years later some of the most distinguished wrote a public letter expressing the deep thanks of all the refugees for their welcome here so long ago, which gave them the chance of a new life.

The checks and procedures at the English Channel ports were so different from the interviews he had had to undertake eleven years ago in Vienna, John thought. It had been a terrible job to send back Russian prisoners of war, captured by the Germans. The prisoners had known the fate they faced. In the years after the War Stalin used some of Hitler's concentration camps in eastern Germany for his own purposes and the number of those dying in them each week increased. His vast Gulag in Russia was too small for his Terror as he began to plan for a Third World War.

'Yes, Hitler did win the War in the shape of Stalin,' John thought.

Here in Folkestone it was all so different. The welcome was so warm that the young Hungarian men believed that the smiling English girls were trying to pick them up. They were surprised and puzzled when they learnt that this was not so; that a smiling, pretty face meant a welcome from the country as a whole, and not something more personal, at least for the moment.

It was the beginning of their English education for the young Hungarians.

Back in Battle, in the Durham family, Giori learned quickly. So did Helena, but there was something specially committed about Giori.

Giori was nearly fourteen years old that autumn. He knew little English. Many Hungarian children of their age (Helena was two years younger) found it difficult to settle and learn the language at first. But, of the twenty thousand who came to Britain in 1956 and 1957, not many had a teacher or a step-father like Mr Durham. As soon as possible after confirmation of the deaths of Eva and Tibor got through the Iron Curtain, John and Barbara adopted Giori and Helena.

Most Hungarian refugees in Britain wished never to hear or speak the Russian language again. Who could blame them? Giori was quite different. He was detached. He did not blame the Russian people for what had happened. He was now hearing a lot about Andrei from the others, especially from Helena.

'It's the Communist system and government that caused it all,' he said. 'Now we're here we can say it openly. It's Communism; it's nothing to do with Russia. They've suffered from it much longer than we have in Hungary.'

Already Giori felt driven to explain this to all those in Great Britain who had no inkling of the calamity that had befallen Russia in 1917 and Eastern Europe after 1945 because of Communism. He spent evenings with John Durham, switching from Hungarian to Russian to English, discussing what had happened and why. He was old for his years.

At school Giori quickly caught up with his English contemporaries and they accepted him.

In the early days the boys expected Giori to be a football genius. In 1953 the Hungarian football team, the Magyars, had beaten England 6-3 at Wembley, England's first defeat at home. The following spring Hungary had won an even greater victory in Budapest, 7-1.

But, although he tried, Giori did not make a footballer. Amazingly, he took to cricket.

'The only Magyar medium pace bowler,' he called himself. In 1959, when he took his pre-sixth-form exams, Giori was captain of the school's junior cricket team. For months no rain fell. Wide cracks opened on the playing filed.

'It is a Hungarian summer,' he told his team. To celebrate he scored a century. 'My brother, Tibor, would have been a spin bowler, just like Jim Laker, I think. How he would have loved it.'

Cricket appealed to Giori because the game lasted so long, and there was such scope for devising a strategy. He was not one to be carried away by apparent success or failure or by anything at all. He laid his plans and stuck to them.

'I will leave school after the sixth form and become a journalist,' he told John one day.

'You could easily get into my college at Oxford, Giori. You would do better than me.' But John knew that nothing would change his mind.

The headmaster also encouraged him to go to university, but Giori was keen to start work soon. He wanted to begin, in some way, to repay the Durhams for all they had done for him and Helena. He said nothing about that. He knew that they wished for no return for their generosity. Giori knew that they would be embarrassed if he told them what he felt. In a way he was also doing it for Tibor.

Giori relished that English sense of embarrassment, and he shared it. He did brilliantly in his A-levels (English, History and French, with Russian done privately with John because the school offered no Russian classes). He felt embarrassed by his success, but was pleased that John and Barbara were so proud of him.

West Germany and West Berlin

IN August 1961 John and Barbara took the family on a special holiday to celebrate Giori's success and his leaving school. It was the first time that Giori and Helena had been back on the Continent since their escape nearly six years ago. There was no question of visiting Hungary although the tension had eased there. The Hungarian people lived a sullen, quiet life, pretending that the uprising had never taken place. It was a pretence that their rulers required of them, a pretence that they gladly accepted for their own peace of mind. The Durhams had no wish to go there. Anyway, they felt it would be unsafe. But in Berlin they would be less than two hundred miles from the border with Czechoslovakia, which was one of Hungary's neighbours.

The whole family was amazed to see how rich the people were in West Germany, how well dressed they were, what shining, sleek cars they drove. John had told them all about the poverty in German cities only sixteen years earlier.

'At the end of the War widows and orphans lived in bombed out cellars,' he remembered. 'They were almost starving. We sent them food though we had severe rationing at home. Everyone in Germany was sunk in defeat and despair.'

'How hard they have worked,' he thought, as they travelled the new German roads (better than anything in Britain, and with many more cars) and visited the rich shops in the town centres.

They caught the sealed, guarded train from West Germany to Berlin which ran for 200 miles through East Germany. Their passports were examined carefully. The East German guards looked at Giori and Helena curiously. Although they now spoke perfect English they looked so different from their sister and parents. Giori looked back steadily but not aggressively at the guard, confident in the value of his blue British passport. Helena slipped her arm through Giori's to distract him.

Through the window, as the train pulled steadily through the East German countryside, they observed the small towns and villages, and the peasants working in the fields.

'Exactly like Hungary,' said Helena.

'Nothing has changed,' said Giori.

What they found in Berlin was a great shock. Millions of marks and dollars had been poured into the western half of the city. It made the contrast with the grey, deprived eastern sector even more shocking.

Two years after the Durhams had been there on holiday, President Kennedy made an official visit to

West Berlin. 'I am a Berliner too,' he declared. The crowd rose and cheered him. Kennedy meant that the West would never abandon Berlin to the Soviet Union, whatever the cost. This had already been proved in 1949 when the Soviet Union closed the railway line and road from West Germany. For months the NATO allies transported all the city's needs to it by plane in an immense airlift around the clock. Eventually, Stalin acknowledged defeat and lifted the blockade.

The intensity of life on the front line between East and West produced a torrid atmosphere in West Berlin.

'There's something sickly about it,' Margaret said. 'It feels like the dollops of cream they put in coffee and serve with the cakes in the cafes.'

None of them liked the fevered life of West Berlin, but the pinched, harsh drabness of the East was worse. There was a steady trickle of refugees crossing into the western sector to prove it. That summer the trickle was growing because of rumours that the Soviet Union was planning to close the border with the West.

People were desperate to get away while they could.

'They look a bit like us, on our way to get into Dodi's lorry.' Helena suddenly took hold of Giori's hand.

'The whole country will escape if they are allowed to.' Giori was looking at the men and women, each carrying a cardboard suitcase. 'The Soviet Union won't let that happen. East Germany is too important for them. They will close the border, and they'll do it soon.'

East Berlin

A MILE or two to the east, on the other side of Berlin, sat Andrei, guarding a pile of luggage that belonged to a small group of Russian 'Pioneers', teenagers like him but all a couple of years younger. The group's holiday in East Germany was nearly over.

Almost all children in Soviet schools joined the Pioneer organisation. The Soviet state allowed no other youth groups. Cubs and brownies, scouts and guides had all been banned by Lenin. Their promises to serve God and humanity in general, regardless of class, did not suit his ideology of class war. All but the working class he regarded as subhuman. The Russian Orthodox Church was not allowed to organise any activities for young people. In the 1950s Khrushchev closed two thirds of the few hundred churches still open.

During the long school holiday in July and August, the Pioneers arranged outings and camps. Usually these were in the Soviet Union, but older members might be taken to the safe, Communist countries of Eastern Europe. Andrei was coming to the end of his time in the Pioneers. He was helping

Tanya, his group's leader, to run this trip to East Germany.

In the five years since his visit the Durhams had received a little news of Andrei. After the crushing of the uprising in Hungary they were afraid what might happen to him and his family, but over the years Andrei had sent them two New Year cards. In return they sent him two cards. They often wondered about his life in Moscow, especially Giori and Helena.

'What happened to Mother and Tibor and Hungary is not Andrei's fault, or his family's, or his people's,' Giori often said. 'It's the system there. The Russians didn't choose it. Lenin and Trotsky and the other bandits and criminals forced it on them. They snuffed out the hope of democracy in Russia... Their successors still terrorise them... Poor Russia.'

John and Barbara agreed, but John did not try to organise any further holiday exchanges with schools behind the Iron Curtain. The two of them concentrated on bringing up their new, big family, and always hoped that one day real news of Andrei would arrive. In those days many people lived like that, hoping for some scrap of news from beyond the Iron Curtain.

In fact, Andrei's family did not suffer because of his visit to Great Britain. Andrei himself flourished at school. His English language raced ahead, and he was just as good at German. It was because of this that he was included in the Pioneer trip to East Germany.

Life there was easier than in Moscow but there was a tension in the air. Andrei's party was mostly kept away from Germans, but they sensed that the population was unsettled. Andrei heard rumours about the huge political demonstrations that had taken place for a short while in East Germany in 1953 after Stalin's death and in Poland in the summer of 1956. Since then East Germany had been quiet, but now people were agitated again.

Like Giori and Helena in the west of the city, Andrei saw people with shabby cardboard suitcases abandoning their homes. He began to count them. The number increased day by day, and those leaving looked more worried and furtive.

As the last few days of Andrei's holiday passed, the group saw lorries carrying building materials and scaffolding. There were many troop-carriers, each with its platoon of nervous young Russian men, their white faces brilliant in the sun against their rough dark uniforms. There was peace on the streets, with no sign of tanks or groups of soldiers marching.

Andrei's group occasionally caught a glimpse of Western life through West German television which many people watched in East Berlin. For the most part they spent their time walking, swimming, visiting historic sites and hearing the story of the Second World War and the capture of Berlin by the Soviet Army in 1945.

As Andrei and the others sat among their luggage waiting for a bus to take them from their hostel to the railway station, their leader Tanya appeared and called them together.

Tanya had been relaxed for most of the holiday, as soon as Anton, her colleague from Moscow disappeared. All the children knew that he was a KGB officer, just from the timid way Tanya treated him and his cool confidence. His work was to make sure that their journey went smoothly, that the East Germans who received them behaved properly and that none of his group, including Tanya herself, showed signs of wishing to escape to the West. It was an easy job. Tanya's husband was back in Moscow, and all of the children were chosen because their family links were strong. The KGB had spent months studying the files of their parents and grandparents for any indication of unreliability.

As soon as they were in Berlin, Anton disappeared. He had some more important work to do. He was an expert on Germany and spoke the language like a native.

Tanya relaxed. She was a teacher of German and English. Although her German was nothing like as fluent as Anton's, her sympathies were much wider and more genuine. For Anton, his skill at the language was just a means to an end, something to use to manipulate people and events to achieve his ends, the ends of his hidden masters. Tanya was different. She had absorbed much of the culture of Germany and its history before the disasters of the last sixty years.

Occasionally, her references to Great Britain showed Andrei that she had a feeling for that country, too, although she had never been there.

Tanya knew that Andrei's parents worked at the university and she had heard Akademik Dmitry lecture once while she was at the Pedagogical Institute during her training as a teacher. Although he liked her, Andrei did not tell her that he had met the Academician. Tanya almost began to treat Andrei as a friend.

'What did you see of London, Andrei?' she asked him.

And, 'Did the people seem tense or relaxed on the streets?'

And even, 'Did the family you were with speak openly to you? Did you see their television?'

Andrei was the only member of the group who had visited a Western country. He could not now believe that the visit had taken place, but it had. It seemed a dream, a miracle. Even Tanya had only ever visited East Germany. Somehow Andrei knew that she was not trying to test his loyalty to Russia or to prove that he was some danger or threat as Anton would have done. They had all edged away from him.

But now, as she rejoined her group, Tanya was not relaxed. All trace of expression had left her face.

'Our plans are changed,' she told her group. 'We are to be flown to Moscow. There are spare spaces on a military plane and the trains are needed by others.'

Tanya continued in a monotone, not looking directly at any of the group gathered around her.

'The government of the German Democratic Republic and the Soviet Authorities in Berlin are taking steps to prevent the West from exploiting the open border between East and West in Berlin. The West is using this border to threaten all the Socialist countries and Russia, to send spies against us, to undermine our way of life. A new entry regime is being created to stop this...

'Now we shall wait for our bus.'

No one spoke, but Andrei understood what it meant. A wall was to be built to divide East from West Berlin. Everyone would pretend that it was designed to keep out the West and its agents and stop them from destroying the way of life in the East. But everyone would know that its purpose was to prevent people with a few belongings stuffed in shabby suitcases from crossing to the West and making their lives there. The activity of the lorries was clear now. Materials for building the wall had been moved up to the boundary between the Soviet sector of Berlin and the Western sectors.

It was on this morning that frantic building work began.

Andrei began carefully to write the second of the two postcards that he had bought. Anna and Yegor, Andrei's special friends – their fathers worked with his – were writing postcards to their families. Andrei's first card was to his parents. They would be spending their holiday with Babushka now at the dacha. Andrei would go there to join them when he got to Moscow.

But Andrei was now writing the second card, to the Durhams. He guarded their address in his heart, and when he thought of them (he often did) he recited it to himself. It was almost a prayer, a link with them that must not be broken.

> I send my greetings to all three of you,
> not forgetting Helena and Tibor.
> I have been on holiday in the GDR and Berlin.
>
> Your A.
>
> P.S. I have seen lots of building works here.

Andrei knew that all mail going to the West would be examined. His card might never reach England. He had no idea what had became of Tibor and Helena, or whether the Durhams were still in touch with them. He just knew that this was what he had to do, however futile it might be. He hoped that somehow Tibor and Helena would receive his message in Hungary. He wanted them to know that not all Russians were monsters despite what had happened to their country. Andrei wrote the postscript to indicate that he knew about the wall. He did it in such a way that the censor reading the card might be able to interpret it as a reference to all the building developments and progress in East Germany. If he were able to take it that way, the official would probably let the card through. Such ambiguities made life possible.

Andrei did not know the price of a stamp to send a card to England. He put all his remaining stamps on it and slipped it into a post box with all the cards written by the rest of the group as the bus arrived.

As Andrei's party made its way to the airport, their bus was once or twice turned away from sensitive areas. They caught glimpses of lorries and soldiers blocking roads, entering houses and removing the families who lived in them.

Soon breeze blocks and barbed wire would block the roads. Bricks would fill the windows which looked out onto the Western sectors. A cordon would be created, a 'no man's land' empty of all life except guards and dogs. And during those days when the wall was being built, some desperate souls would escape and others would die in the attempt. The flood would ease to a trickle, and still people would try to escape. Some would tunnel. Others would go mad and simply try to climb the barbed wire. They would be shot in the back by the guards on the east.

For this was a matter of life and death for a system, for the Soviet empire.

The Berlin Wall would stand there for twenty-eight years. It would dominate the life of Europe and the world.

Sussex

WHEN they got back to Battle, Giori picked up the letters and bills lying on the doormat. After the holidays it was always Giori who led them to the front door, striding ahead, amazed at the greenness of English grass, and how much it had grown in the two weeks they had been away, so unlike the parched gardens of Hungary in August.

'A card from Andrei,' he told the others and handed it to Barbara. 'He was there the same day as us, the day the wall began to go up.'

Giori showed her the postmark.

'He doesn't know that I'm here... He doesn't know about Tibor... He doesn't know that Giori is here,' said Helena. 'And it's too risky to tell him.'

'He saw the wall going up,' said Margaret. 'Just like us, but from the other side. You were right, Giori. They wouldn't let the people go on escaping like that. Now there'll be no contact at all. We may never see Andrei again.'

Immediately she regretted expressing her fear.

'We shall,' said Helena. 'Remember how he learnt to swim and surf. He'd never been in the sea before.

Remember how he and Tibor used to race into the water... One day we shall see him.'

Helena often talked to Margaret about Tibor. It was a way of keeping him alive in their memory. Giori had entrusted to her the little handkerchief of Hungarian soil and she kept it in her bedroom beside the album of photographs that John and Barbara had made up for her of their first holiday together. Another small photograph of Tibor stood on her bedside table.

'The wall won't stop it. Somehow we'll manage. The wall will come down. We'll see Andrei,' she repeated, blushing at how vehemently she was speaking.

Giori bit his lip hard and looked away. He caught John's eye. Neither of them spoke.

1962-1967
Sussex and London

GIORI joined *The Courier*, a local weekly newspaper in Sussex as a reporter. He covered everything: cases in magistrates' courts, agricultural and vegetable shows, cricket, even football.

'Giori has an article on every other page this week,' Barbara would often find herself saying to friends and neighbours. She and John were proud of him. 'He writes better English than all the others.'

After a year or so, Giori had a lucky break. He was playing cricket on a late summer afternoon in September for his team at Battle. The rest of the family was there to watch him.

John introduced Giori to an old friend, Andrew Palmer, who worked at the BBC. Andrew had served with John in the Army in Vienna in 1945. He had a talk with Giori. They discussed the crisis building up in Cuba, where the Soviet Union was beginning to send medium and long range missiles.

'The Americans must turn back the ships carrying the Soviet missiles,' Giori said. 'If they are installed in Cuba, no one will be safe. Khrushchev has said that he wants to bury us. We must take him at his word and stop him...President Kennedy must stop them now, while it is still possible. It is the only way.'

'But the Soviet leaders will never accept that,' said Mr Palmer. 'Cuba is their only Communist ally in the West.'

'Khrushchev will accept it,' said Giori. 'He will back down. Until those missiles are there, the Americans are much stronger, and the Soviet Union is thousands of miles from Cuba... He will back down. It is the only language they respect: consistency and power. Nothing else counts with them...

'We learnt that in Hungary,' he added quietly. 'Khrushchev has already buried my mother and brother...'

A wicket fell. Giori went in to bat. Mr Palmer watched him score a determined, elegant fifty and win the match for his side. He was thoughtful on the train back to Charing Cross.

Helena did not speak much to Mr Palmer, but she was listening carefully and was sure that what Giori said was right. It was not only what Hungary had suffered that convinced them both and all the family, but also what they had seen together the previous year in Berlin. Helena had a feeling that this conversation was somehow important for Giori's future.

Andrew Palmer was working at the BBC on the Sunday evening at the end of October when the news came through that Khrushchev had ordered the Soviet ships to turn back from Cuba, in the face of President

Kennedy's quarantine of the island. America's overwhelming power in the West caused the Soviet Union to dismantle its missile sites on Cuba and to return the equipment to Russia.

That evening Andrew telephoned John and asked for Giori's telephone number. Giori was by now living in a small flat in Battle, while Helena continued to live with the Durhams as she and Margaret prepared for their A-levels.

A month later Giori started to work in London at Bush House, the headquarters of the overseas services of the BBC. Its news service was at that time respected by everyone for its honesty and accuracy as it would be for many years to come.

Giori became a trainee foreign affairs analyst and linguist. Soon he moved to London to share a flat there with some young colleagues, but the Durhams' house would always be his home.

Another school-leaver from John's school took over the reporting of court cases and village shows for *The Courier*.

Giori did well. Over the next few years his voice became well known in Hungarian and Russian to hundreds of thousands of the BBC's listeners from Budapest to Moscow and far beyond. Giori had fallen on his feet.

'My work is my university,' he said. He had no regrets.

Margaret and Helena both went to Oxford, but to

different colleges, Helena to Somerville and Margaret to St Anne's. Oxford life suited them.

The Durham's big house seemed empty and quiet in term, but in the vacations Giori sometimes came to stay with them and it was like old times with all five of them together.

Suddenly, John felt ten or twenty years younger as he spent hours in discussion with Giori. They would go swimming at Birling Gap or walking on the South Downs with a picnic. Then they would return home and eat an enormous meal cooked by Barbara and the girls, sitting in the garden as the fragrance of the tall white tobacco plants drifted over them.

'If only Tibor...,' said Barbara. They spoke of him often, and doing so somehow kept him alive with them.

'And Andrei,' said Margaret quietly, looking at Helena.

Come October, and with it the beginning of Helena and Margaret's last year at Oxford, it would seem so quiet and lonely again for John and Barbara. That was the price of such happiness.

Russia

A$_T$ the time when Margaret and Helena were preparing for their last year at Oxford, Andrei graduated at the Moscow State Institute of International Relations.

By now he knew much more about the Soviet invasion of Hungary in 1956. From his school he had won his place at the Institute against fierce competition from school leavers all over the Soviet Union. Most of the students at the Institute were children of the elite in the Communist Party, the *Nomenklatura*, those with access to special privileges. A tiny number of places each year were reserved for open competition. Andrei's father had never been more than a nominal Party member, the bottom rung which enabled him to keep his academic job, but Andrei's brilliance and his almost perfect English and German won him his place.

Some of the students at the Institute would go on to become Party leaders. Others became KGB officers, spotted as having the necessary qualities by the KGB staff working in the Institute and destined to serve abroad. Others would become normal diplomats, and it was this career on which Andrei, for good or ill, set his heart and in his last year he was recruited by the Ministry of Foreign Affairs. He had to become a nominal member of the Party.

The library at the Institute included books which were found almost nowhere else in Russia. Andrei began to read the accounts of Russian and Soviet history given in English and German books.

Many of the books were written by Communists or fellow travellers from Western countries. Lenin called them 'useful idiots', useful for deceiving non-Communists and in spreading Soviet propaganda.

'Are they fools or are they just wicked or are they in the KGB's pay?' Andrei asked himself as he read their books. 'They live in freedom but they've let themselves be corrupted. What makes them spread lies for the Communist cause?'

Andrei felt frightened by the power and scale of Soviet deceit and his country's will to spread revolution around the world. He withdrew into himself and hid what he was learning and the views that he was forming.

He devoured the works of more detached German, British or American authors. The opportunity might well not come his way again. He learnt for the first time the full story of the events which had taken place in Hungary a few weeks after his return from England in 1956, and much more.

Andrei could not believe his luck as he walked from the metro station to his office in the Ministry on the first Monday in September 1967. In Smolenskaya Square he passed through the tall, heavy, wooden doors of the immense building, over five hundred feet high. A Stalinist wedding cake, people called it.

Andrei's life changed for ever. He became an official, required to fit in with the rules, many written, but more of them unwritten. He would enjoy the privileges of meeting foreigners and of living abroad. He would have access to foreign currency and be able to buy foreign goods. He would have to represent the official Soviet line despite all he had learnt about it.

At work in Moscow Andrei never spoke of all he had learnt from Babushka and discovered in his years at the Institute. He knew that some of the other young men who joined the Ministry with him had read the same books. Some might share his views. But it hung over him that the KGB had recruited others among them to report on their colleagues. Andrei was careful. He held his peace.

The weeks and months passed. A new year came.

1968
Edinburgh

'THERE are our seats, Helena,' said Margaret. She pointed to the back row of the gallery, just below the windows near the roof of the church.

Helena led the way up the steep stairs as the audience settled down for the concert. She and Margaret squeezed along their row, apologising to people who had already taken their seats.

'Just in time,' said Helena.

The two of them were having a music holiday together to celebrate their graduation. After concerts in Edinburgh at the Festival they were to go back to London and attend a couple of Proms.

They joined the audience in clapping as a tall, slim man in his fifties, carrying his violin, walked to a platform far below them. He was to give a concert of music by Bach and Paganini.

Yehudi Menuhin stood still on the platform.

'I would like to dedicate this concert to the people of Czechoslovakia,' he said.

The audience was silent for a minute. It seemed

that all their concentrated thoughts and perhaps prayers were poured into that minute.

Margaret put her arm around Helena and held her gently.

'Mother and Tibor,' said Helena. 'Now there will be more families torn apart like ours.'

Yehudi Menuhin gestured to the audience to sit. He began to play a partita by Bach.

On that cool August afternoon the sound of the violin rose and fell and soared again, carrying the audience's spirits with it. Movement followed movement, and through it violinist and listeners entered into the hopes and despair of a small, peaceful people whose leaders had told them not to fight, not to resist the tanks that were now rolling in from the East, tanks manned by troops from the Soviet Union, East Germany, Poland, and, worst of all for Helena, from Hungary. The Hungarian people, which had risen twelve years ago against their oppressors, and had been united in a vain attempt to win freedom, was now compelled to drive its tanks across the border from Budapest into Czechoslovakia and crush another people's hopes.

Prague

ALL spring, as Margaret and Helena had worked hard for their final examinations, they had shared the hopes of the Czechs and Slovaks for peaceful change in their country. The 'Prague Spring', it was called.

The new leader of the Czechoslovak Communist Party, Mr Dubcek, became a familiar face in newspapers and on the television as he and his government tried to introduce what he called 'Communism with a human face.'

The press in Czechoslovakia was freed from control by the state and the Communist Party. Public debate was allowed. Reform was in the air. Mr Dubcek and the Czechoslovaks never spoke or thought of leaving the Warsaw Pact, controlled by the Soviet Union, or of becoming a neutral country. Many people thought that it was because of those dreams that Hungary's uprising had been crushed. No one wanted that to happen again.

The West behaved cautiously. There was no rhetoric from governments about 'the rights of the subject peoples of Eastern Europe', as there had been in 1956, only to be followed by the betrayal of those who had believed the speeches. Anyway, the

Americans had an unending war of their own to deal with, in Vietnam, as doomed to failure as the Suez expedition had been.

The Prague Spring was just the hope of a small nation, loyal to Moscow, to Communism and to the Warsaw Pact trying to introduce 'Communism with a human face.'

London

GIORI did not share the Western public's hopes and he was unmoved by the spirit of optimism and change which intoxicated the world in 1968.

'Those were the days, my friend; we thought they'd never end': Mary Hopkin's hit song rang out later that summer from every radio set, but Giori was not carried away.

'All days are the same for them,' he said. 'They will not allow even the little freedom that poor Mr Dubcek wants.

'It is against their tradition. It is against the Soviet tradition... There can be no Communism with a human face. In Moscow they know it and do not care. They will not allow it.'

Month after month in the spring and summer of 1968 he was hard at work at the BBC analysing what was happening and what was being written in the papers and said by people in Czechoslovakia and Russia. He travelled frequently to Prague and Vienna, and broadcast reports from there. He never changed his opinion.

'They will not allow it. It is just a matter of time.'

Many celebrated historians and economists, experts in international relations and in the history of the Communist countries came to the BBC to broadcast their views as the events unfolded. Many of them seemed to Giori to be indulging in wishful thinking. Some may have been in the pay of the KGB. He listened to them carefully and talked with them and learnt much from them about individual events and people. But few of them seemed to grasp the full picture.

'They were not there, so they cannot understand what it all means. They have not been through it. You have to go through it, to see their faces as they invade your country, to understand it.'

Giori thought this often as he travelled from the Home Service at Broadcasting House in Langham Place to Bush House in the Strand for the General Overseas Service and the Hungarian and Russian Services.

He said the same to the Durhams when he visited them on days off, which became a rarity as the months passed. Continually Giori was being called in to work to deal with emergencies.

There was just one visiting commentator, Geza, who openly shared Giori's views to the full. He was a Hungarian.

'"Gaze-ah," he used to say, 'not "geezer",' when people had trouble with his name.

One day, after a broadcast when Geza had argued with two professors, from British and American universities, that a Soviet invasion was inevitable, he had a cup of coffee with Giori in the BBC canteen.

'They just can't see it,' said Giori.

'It's as if they're colour-blind,' replied Geza. 'They see all the details and know so many facts, but they can't make sense of the outlines and shapes; none of the meaning of it all is there for them.'

Geza was almost twice Giori's age, but his manner was boyish and enthusiastic.

'In a way, we were lucky to see it for ourselves. There is no substitute,' Giori went on. 'My mother's death, and Tibor's, made it all clear.'

Geza's father had been a Hungarian Communist, a friend of Lenin's. He had been a leader of the short-lived revolution in Budapest in 1918. When that failed he fled to Moscow with his wife.

Geza had been born and educated in Moscow. His family had been respected for its efforts to spread the revolution across Europe. Lenin's ambition was to encourage Communist revolutions in all Europe, even in Great Britain, and as soon as possible. He thought that, unless Europe, even all the world, turned Communist, his revolution in Russia was doomed to fail. Foreign revolutionaries like Geza's parents were honoured by Lenin. They were to be his agents to impose Bolshevik power around the globe. In the meantime they lived lives of great privilege in Moscow.

But in 1938, when Geza was seventeen, his father was taken and interrogated by the Soviet secret police. He disappeared. Geza and his mother survived. Geza became a university teacher of history. In 1957, after his mother's death, he and his wife were sent to Africa to work at a university, in one of the countries that became independent as the British Empire ended. Geza was charged by his bosses to work for the Soviet cause in the country and to encourage Communists at the university where he was lecturing. Many of the Communists in the university were in the pay of the Soviet Communist Party or the KGB.

Geza became sickened by the task of trying to reduce the influence of Great Britain in its former colony, in the favour of the Soviet Union.

'It was clearly not a change for the better,' Geza would explain in later years.

He loved understatement even more than the British did. It was one of the features that attracted him to the country in the first place and helped form a strong bond with Giori when they met at the BBC in 1968.

Geza and his wife had fled to Britain about ten years earlier and sought political asylum. In London he lost all the privileges he had enjoyed in Moscow, but his brilliance won him a post as a lecturer at a university. He became a natural, engaging broadcaster. His contributions were controversial and profound. Although everything he said was against the spirit of the times ('easy optimism,' he called it, 'with no attention to history'), he was popular even with those who disagreed with him.

'There will be no change,' said Geza, 'until they decide not to use force to maintain their rule. It all depends on their willingness to kill people. I don't mean people in Asia or in the far extremities of the

Soviet Union. All empires behave in the same way, far away from home. It is a matter of degree between the various empires. The Americans are willing to kill in Vietnam, and to use torture there, but the Russians are far worse.

'I mean, are the Russians willing to kill in Europe and in European Russia? As long as they are willing to kill those who dare to go on strike in Russia or put writers and dissidents in prison and labour camps and torture them and to shoot people protesting for freedom in Eastern Europe, there will be no end of Communism.'

'The use of terror is inseparable from Bolshevism,' replied Giori, quoting Lenin. 'How can they ever stop?'

Geza snorted in delight at Giori's accurate knowledge of Lenin's words.

'At the moment, they are willing to kill as many as they must so as to hold on to power. If we ever see them hesitate in Europe, then we shall know that the end is near.

'"Learn a parable of the fig tree. When her branch is yet tender, and putteth forth leaves, ye know that summer is near. So ye in like manner, when ye see these things come to pass know that it is nigh, even at the doors."'

Geza was Jewish and devoutly observed his faith. He loved to shock his non-Jewish friends in Britain and Western Europe by quoting the words of Jesus from the New Testament which he knew and respected more than most of them did.

'So far, I see no sign of the change we're looking for,' Geza continued. 'If anything, the repression is growing worse in Russia. Authors are being put on trial in Moscow, dissidents are sent for psychiatric treatment, censorship is growing even stricter, and there is worse persecution of religious believers. How can they let the Prague Spring become a Prague Summer? It would be the beginning of the end for them. They will not accept it.'

'Those professors couldn't see it,' said Giori. 'It's as if their great learning has killed their commonsense.'

'"Your great learning is driving you mad, Paul,"' Geza quoted gleefully from the *Acts of the Apostles*.

'They believe that things are changing gradually there,' he went on. 'And some things *are* changing. Living standards will get worse as they spend more and more on arms. But the *main thing* cannot change slowly. It's like a river breaking up at the end of winter. One day it looks like solid ice, and the next day it's all crashing and splitting, and sweeping out to the sea. The change that matters is invisible to us all. It's their willingness to kill so as to hold on to power. One day, perhaps, their leaders will not want to do that, and then it'll all be over, quicker than we can imagine. Suddenly it'll be as if the ice had never been there.'

'If we're right, it means that none of us will be able to forecast the end,' said Giori. 'The pessimists and the optimists, and the academics and the politicians and the intelligence services, all of us will get it wrong, and we'll curse ourselves for not spotting in advance the thing we've all devoted our lives to.'

'It'll be the final refutation of Marx, as well as the end of Lenin's system,' said Geza. 'It can only end when one person, or a group, or the Generals in the Red Army, decide not to use their weapons to hold down their people in a system that no one can really believe in any more. But it'll be a decision by one person or a small group to end the system of government by terror. Their economic system is a disaster, but the end of all that horror won't be caused by economic forces...

'It'll depend on the Russian people and the other peoples of Eastern Europe responding and taking advantage of the crisis. Only the people there can do that...

'It will be a moral thing. Only those tuned in to goodness and truth, determined not to live by lies, will have any chance of forecasting it. Not many of those, I fear...

'"The wind bloweth where it listeth, and thou hearest the sound thereof, but canst not tell whence it cometh and whither it goeth."'

Giori laughed.

'... Or it will be a mistake,' Geza continued, carried away by the chance to tell the whole story without interruption. 'One of their leaders may not realise that relaxing the terror will finish Bolshevism. If the Russian people or the peoples of Eastern Europe realise *that*, they will lose their fear and rise against their rulers. Whichever it is, none of us will predict it.

'But until I see a slight movement in the ice, or feel the warmth of the breeze moving "where it listeth",

I shall not change my views. And so far there's no sign. The winter of repression in Moscow is getting more severe, if anything. Everything depends on Moscow, not on Prague. The reformers, poor Mr Dubcek, will be swept away in Prague as soon as Moscow's fears get too strong, just as you were in Hungary.'

They finished their coffee. Before they could leave the building to go home they were called back to the studio for another crisis broadcast.

Russia

DAY by day in Moscow Andrei followed the events of the Prague Spring. Early in the morning and late in the evening after work he tuned in to the BBC's Russian Service and the American station, Radio Liberty.

In those years Soviet factories still produced huge numbers of short wave radio sets so that people could receive Radio Moscow's broadcasts from end to end of their vast country. In the 1970s, as the repression of all independent or dissident thought got even worse, fewer sets were manufactured. Television took over in Russia. The fewer the short wave sets there were, the less the population was able to hear news from the West.

Despite the noisy interference broadcast by Soviet transmitters to jam foreign wavelengths, Andrei often managed to hear the news from London about what was happening in Czechoslovakia. Occasionally he heard short reports by Giori. Even on the short wave radio, Andrei could detect that Giori's fluent Russian was delivered with a slight Hungarian and slighter English accent. He had no idea that Giori was Helena's brother, although they shared the same surname. Although the Durhams had adopted them, Giori used his old Hungarian surname for his broadcasts.

Andrei liked Giori's reports. He could tell that he was only a few years older than him. What Giori said was sharp and realistic, but not cynical or world-weary. He felt that Giori was speaking for those who were not carried away by foolish optimism or dreams, for those who knew how little could be achieved. He guessed that this must owe a lot to what had happened in Hungary in 1956.

Only at the dacha, alone with Babushka, in the silence of the Russian countryside, did Andrei speak about what he had learnt over the years. He trusted Babushka completely. He knew that, at her age, he could not endanger her and that she would never tell anyone his secrets.

'Nothing can justify what the Communists did to us.' Babushka was giving Andrei a cup of tea at breakfast.

Andrei called her his 'real teacher.' She had been seventeen years old when the Bolsheviks seized power. From her own experience of normal Russian life before Lenin's *coup d'etat*, which ousted by force of arms the revolutionary government set up in March, she knew directly what Andrei and his parents had to struggle to understand. This contrast gave her a horror of what had happened in Russia. Andrei wanted to learn as much as possible from her before it was too late.

In the early May of that year of the Prague Spring, Andrei spent a few days alone with Babushka at the dacha. He was recovering from influenza.

Every year, like hundreds of thousands of Russians, Andrei's family opened up their dacha for the May Day celebrations and the holiday on the ninth of May which marked the defeat of Nazi Germany in 1945. By then it was mild enough to live there and work on the vegetable plot. For the few days between the two holidays Andrei and Babushka were alone together.

As they got ready to work in the garden, Andrei began to speak of what he was learning of the history of their country.

'That visit to England, and then the uprising in Hungary and our invasion were landmarks for me.'

'Landmark is a good word,' replied Babushka. 'When I was a girl a group of Russian philosophers wrote a book called *Landmarks*. Scholars like that were all swept away by the Bolsheviks... You are learning so much.'

'But you've lived through it all,' said Andrei. 'You saw it with your own eyes from the beginning.'

'Your parents' generation suffered most,' said Babushka. 'They were born into the terror that Lenin began. They were born under it. They are good people but now they are too old to change... At least I had those seventeen years before the Communists stole our country from us all. Perhaps you will live to see it end...'

They worked together quietly, steadily digging a

trench in the soil and carefully putting the seed potatoes in it.

Around them the silver birch trees were coming into leaf. The sound of the wind could be heard in the upper boughs, but all else was silence. Ilya's family's dacha, visible faintly through the pale green leaves, was still closed up and deserted. Their life was a mystery to Andrei nowadays. He had not met Ilya since they left school. The sun was comfortingly warm in the intense Russian spring, soon to transform the countryside during the short summer growing season.

'You think it may end one day?' Andrei asked her.

'It must. It is all based on lies and force. God will not let it last for ever...'

Andrei and Babushka rested from digging and sat next to each other on the old wooden bench in front of the dacha.

'There were many landmarks in my life, too' said Babushka. 'When I was eleven a socialist revolutionary murdered our Prime Minister, Peter Stolypin. It happened in September in Kiev, at the Opera. The Tsar was there but he was not hurt. My family was on holiday in the Crimea. I was swimming every day in the Black Sea. But when my parents heard the news of Stolypin's death, all the holiday spirit left us.

'Father said, "It's the end".

'I could not grasp what he meant. I was too young, but soon it became clear. Stolypin was the last hope. He tried to give land to the peasant farmers, to make them independent and the country rich. After Stolypin died there was no more leadership. Tsar

Nikolai's wife was devoted to him but she was jealous of all his ministers and interfered and caused confusion.'

'Then the war came in August 1914.' Andrei was picking up her thoughts.

'It destroyed Russia's men and spirit and industry,' replied Babushka. 'We were not ready for it. Without it, Lenin and the Bolsheviks would never have succeeded. He knew that. And the Tsarina's fear about her poor son's health made her fall for the tricks of the wicked monk Rasputin, and all the people of Russia lost their faith in the Royal family which had been strong even in 1914.'

'I've read what Lenin wrote,' said Andrei. '"We must turn this Imperialist War into a Civil War in Russia and start a revolution."'

'As a girl of fourteen I heard that a terrorist called Princip shot Archduke Franz Ferdinand in Sarajevo in July 1914. Franz Ferdinand was the heir to the Austro-Hungarian throne, and his murder by a Serb was bound to lead to war and drag us in. The Serbs were such close allies of ours. Some people said later that Princip was secretly acting as Lenin's agent.* The Bolsheviks just wanted to cause chaos and death and get their chance to seize power.'

---

* Twenty-three years later, at his show-trial, Radek blurted out the truth. He was a devoted comrade of Lenin. In his last words at the trial in 1937 he revealed that it was on Lenin's orders and as his agent that Princip shot the Archduke. His brilliant speech is a mass of hidden meanings for the Russian reader and is full of bitter irony against Stalin, hard to convey in English.

'Even Lenin's book and speeches show that he loved war and violence and terrorism and killing people,' said Andrei.

'He certainly hated Russia.' Babushka's head was bowed. 'There was something deranged in his family.'

'He wanted to destroy Russia, just like the Germans,' Andrei replied. 'Lenin hated our people. "Russian fools", he called us. "If you want to get anything done, get some Germans", that's what he said. It's all there to read in his books.'

'It's true,' said Babushka. 'One of his most trusted friends, Margarita Fofanova, told me how close his links were with the Germans.

'I met Margarita in Leningrad in the 1930s. She hid Lenin in her flat for the fortnight just before the Bolsheviks seized power.

'In the 1920s she became disillusioned with them all. Somehow we got on well, although she must have guessed that I was a religious believer. I spent a day with her. She told me the whole truth about Lenin's time hiding in her flat. He was visited by two German secret agents. The three of them spoke in German together.* Ever since 1914 Lenin had been plotting with the Germans to disrupt Russia and get the Bolsheviks into power there. They gave him huge sums of money to do their dirty work, so that after the

* Margarita Fofanova's personal testimony of Lenin's meeting with German secret agents in her flat was recorded in full, after her death, in *Lenin: the biography of a personality and a politician* by her friend and pupil Akim Arutyunov (2003). The book is available only in Russian as *Lenin: lichnostnaya i politicheskaya biografia*.

coup Lenin would betray our allies, Great Britain and France, and make a separate peace with Germany.

'Margarita was devoted to Lenin, but she wanted me to know that something was wrong, right from the beginning. She may still be alive, but you need to know this, you alone, Andrei. You must know this but keep yourself safe...'

Babushka stood still for a while, looking at the trees and at the rows of potatoes they had planted.

'Lenin's soul was full of cruelty and hatred. He gathered around him the worst men in Russia, one or two of them brilliant, like Trotsky and Bukharin, but all of them the moral dregs of our people. He just attracted the worst men, and women, too. They emptied the prisons. All the most violent, cruel convicts saw that they could make their future in the Bolshevik Party. They could never create anything, only destroy.

'In 1918 there was an attempt to assassinate Lenin. A woman revolutionary was blamed for it. But I remember rumours that the whole story about her was made up and that the plot against him was organised by some Bolshevik leaders who thought that he was too pro-German...

'Anyway, Lenin unleashed the Cheka and started the Red Terror. He'd set it up a few weeks after he had seized power in 1917, and now the orders were given: destroy all opposition, take them and shoot them and hang them, reduce the population to a terror that they'll never recover from.

'And we never have recovered...'

'The Germans helped Lenin seize power and destroy Russia, but it cost them dear. In the 1920s Hitler took to heart the lessons that Lenin taught – how to use power and terror.'

'Nowadays the Party says that if Lenin had lived and Stalin hadn't taken over all would have been well,' said Andrei.

'But things just went on in the direction Lenin had already started,' Babushka replied. 'Perhaps Lenin was the worst of them all. Molotov, Stalin's closest conspirator for more than twenty years, said that Lenin was even harsher and more severe than Stalin himself. He knew what he was talking about. Stalin ordered that Molotov's wife should be imprisoned. Molotov was there when Stalin gave the orders. He just sat there in the room with Stalin and let it happen... A coward and a bully like the rest... Despite that horror, he said that Lenin was *worse* than Stalin. Try to imagine it.'

Babushka rose from the bench where she and Andrei were sitting by the door and together they went back to the vegetable plot. It was half planted by now. They turned the soil and put in the seed potatoes which Babushka had carefully chosen and stored at the end of the last growing season. The work was heavy but they worked in a rhythm, moving along the rows where, last year, they had grown onions and beetroot.

Andrei kept an eye on Babushka, but the old lady

was fit and was enjoying working with her grandson. It was as if Babushka had stored up all these impressions in her heart until the right time came, when Andrei knew enough to take in what she was telling him about how her generation had lived, to understand that this was for him alone, too dangerous to discuss with anyone else. She had even chosen a time when Andrei's parents were not at the dacha so that they would not be implicated in the conversation or compromised. She was speaking for herself, Andrei understood, and for millions of her generation, already dead.

'Akademik Dmitry understood all this,' she said, as if picking up Andrei's thought.

'He lived through it all like you.'

'Yes, and he did nothing except join a literary discussion group. There was never anything political about it or him. They just read and discussed our Old Russian literature. But the Cheka arrested him in Petrograd, well before Lenin's death. He was sent to a concentration camp on an island in the White Sea. It had been a holy monastery until 1917 but the Bolsheviks turned it into a slave camp. He told me he was lucky. They freed him after four years and he returned to the university in Leningrad, and he's worked there all his life. He still works on Old Russian literature and history. It's an escape from the present and a hope for the future, and somehow it helps him understand everything we've endured during this century.'

'He knew that you saw it all, too?'

They took another rest on the bench in the shade.

'Of course, we both lived through it. I lived through it with your grandfather.'

Andrei sat very still, close to Babushka, leaning against her shoulder, supporting her as she spoke of her husband of whom Andrei had heard almost nothing. The birds were silent in the afternoon warmth. The birch trees slept in the sun.

'The NKVD, that's what the secret police was called by then, just came and took him... He never saw your father. It was just before he was born. Your father never speaks of it.'

Babushka sat, her back held erect, and she looked straight ahead.

'Your grandfather was a philosopher, a brilliant man. He had written his first book and it was stored carefully in the drawer of our writing table, waiting for the end of the Civil War to be published. But the end of the Civil War came and things got worse.

'Lenin hated all independent, logical thought. At school he didn't get ten-out-of-ten for logic in his diploma, and even the Communists' records admit it. How they expect us to believe that he got a gold medal at school without that, as they claim, I don't know. They take us for fools about everything...

'Perhaps Lenin hated all thought, all people who used their minds rather than swallowing Bolshevik prejudices and passions. So he decided to get rid of all Russia's best thinkers. He had the list drawn up and he added names to it himself, brilliant, honest people whom he hated, whose honesty and goodness he hated... to imprison some, and to exile others, thousands of them... Philosophers and economists and historians and theologians and scientists, the glory of the universities, the best of the nation, all of them lost to Russia because of Lenin and the Bolsheviks. Lenin replaced them with thugs and bandits.

'Every evening your grandfather prepared a little bag and kept it beside our bed; just a few things he might be allowed to take if the NKVD came for him. Then, when they came and searched the flat and took him, he forgot it. He left it behind and I didn't notice in time. I keep it with me always. Every night I open it and hold his gloves, the gloves he would have needed so much to survive. He is with me...'

Again, Babushka paused and controlled her feelings.

'He had poor health and soon died. Only fifteen years ago, when Stalin died, did they tell me that he died in May 1924, in the Solovetsky prison camp where the Academician was also being held. He remembered your grandfather, of course... They threw him in a common grave.'

Andrei remembered that the Academician had made the sign of the Cross over Babushka and that she had responded in the same way. It was as if Grandfather had entrusted a blessing to his friend which, many years later, Akademik Dmitry had passed on to his wife.

'I made my living by teaching the piano. Your father and I survived. A piano teacher, alone with a growing son, was not of much interest to *them*. I avoided all contact with anyone who might be damaged by me or who might betray me.

'My only aim was that our son should survive; that, and my music. I lost myself in him and in the music. We survived.'

'In Stalin's time...?'

'We saw people disappear. Flats became empty. New people arrived and lived there for a while. They disappeared. Then it would happen all over again.

'We used to see black vans going about Leningrad, taking political prisoners off for imprisonment and torture... They say that the women doing the interrogation were just as bad as the men...

'We were isolated. Children at your father's school disappeared when their parents were arrested and imprisoned or shot. Classes got smaller. There were permanent gaps, empty desks. Teachers disappeared. We had to pretend to each other that it wasn't happening.

'Then, in the evenings your father would read. He was already a brilliant linguist like you.'

Andrei blushed and smiled at Babushka. She continued.

'I would play Bach and Haydn and Mozart. Especially Bach... I transcribed one of Bach's cantatas* from a score your grandfather had always had with him in the flat. It was his favourite. The music and the words helped save me:

* B.W.V. 34.

Blessed are you, chosen souls, whom God hath
    made His dwelling;
Who could find such sure salvation?
Who count the number of his blessings?
And this is the Lord's own doing.

'Thank God for Bach...'

Babushka bowed her head and was silent for a
while. Andrei put his arm gently around her shoulders.

'We kept sane. We did not let Stalin achieve his
final victory and drive us mad. I never forgot that
there had been a real life before war and revolution,
and that Lenin and Stalin and their ideology, their
Party had destroyed us. We were not like this before
them, and Lenin and Stalin and Communism
destroyed us and our beloved country... It is hard to
lose your country.

'Always I hope.'

Babushka's voice was quiet and calm, but there was
a note of triumph in it. She had not been defeated.

For a while they did not speak.

Babushka rose and fetched a piece of sausage and
some bread. They shared it out, each trying to make
sure that the other had more to eat. But Babushka was
insistent.

'You need more,' she said. 'In Leningrad in the
blockade we had a small slice of bread every day.
That's all; if we were lucky.'

They ate a few small apples that had been stored
over the winter, the fruit of the apple trees that
Babushka had grafted and pruned over the years.

'Stalin hated Leningrad,' she said. 'Perhaps he hated all Russia and Russians just as much as Lenin did. Lenin was a mix of five races, German, Swedish and Jewish on his mother's side; Chuvash and Kalmyk – small Asiatic peoples – on his father's. No one dares to say that now but we all knew it in those early days.

'Stalin was from a small people, in the far south, a Georgian; a valiant people in the Caucasus Mountains on the fringes of the Russian Empire. He could not understand Russian traditions and qualities, or the intellectual elite, and he brought shame on his own Georgian people; they did not deserve it. St Petersburg, Leningrad, symbolised everything he hated. He was jealous even of Kirov, the Communist leader in Leningrad. Because Kirov became more popular than him and received too many votes at a Party meeting, Stalin had him murdered in December 1934. It was the beginning of the greatest terror of all, just after your father's birthday.'

'Was Stalin just mad?'

'No, he had a subtle mind. When he was young he wrote poetry, good Georgian poetry that was published. One poem was in the anthology for schoolchildren there for many years.

'He was a brilliant strategist, destroying everyone who might threaten his power. Trotsky and Bukharin underrated him, a ghastly mistake and such a help to him.

'The Army, the secret police, the Party itself — again and again their leaders were purged — arrested, imprisoned, shot. There were public trials of all those who had been Lenin's closest associates.

'They all confessed to errors or to spying or to sabotaging the revolution they had themselves created. What tortures they must have suffered. Perhaps *they* really were mad. Perhaps *they* believed that if they were arrested and interrogated on the orders of the Great Leader of the Party, Lenin's party, that they had worshipped and given their lives to, they must be guilty in some way.

'There were films of their trials, with hysterical condemnations and ecstatic applause from the public when the accused were condemned to death... Wave after wave of killings...'

Andrei and Babushka sat at the table for a while. They had a cup of tea and ate some of last year's strawberry jam from a saucer.

Babushka took a small envelope of little black seeds and sowed them in a wooden potting tray.

'Summer roses, I call them' she said. 'They like growing in pots in the hot sun in July and August. They need a lot of water every day.'

'I've seen them in the flat,' said Andrei.

'We grew them every year, your father and I. Your grandfather loved them. He saw them first in the garden of a peasant family in Karelia who gave him a meal when he was there on holiday as a little boy. He never forgot that holiday or the family...

'All those years together, your father and I were

living there in Leningrad, in our tiny flat, never speaking of all this to each other or to anyone else, year after year, simply trying to survive. He went to school every day. I taught my pupils. We went to concerts. We read. Your grandfather would have been proud of him. Nothing else mattered.

'I have no idea how much your father knew of what was happening. With his languages and books, perhaps he was able to shut most of it out. And now it's too late for him and me to talk like this, too late...

'Perhaps he knows it all himself. Perhaps he doesn't speak to me about it out of reverence or love for his father whom he never knew. Perhaps he spares me the wounds it would tear open in my heart if he spoke of his father.'

Babushka and Andrei got up from the table and went back to the garden. They worked in silence for a long while. There was a comfort in it; in the moist earth, in opening it up and dropping in the potatoes, each with its shoots of new life, the crop that would feed them during the winter in Moscow.

Babushka began to speak again. It was as if she could not stop the flow of her words now that her mind and heart were open. Perhaps it would be her only chance to tell her only grandson the story of her life, of the hidden years of the country which they both loved so much.

'We hoped for a while, at the end of the War, in 1945, that things would improve. We thought that Stalin would give us a breathing space because we had proved ourselves to him. We thought that he would leave open the churches where he had allowed us to worship God together during the War.'

Babushka and Andrei stood at the end of the row they had just planted, bathed in the sunshine pouring through the tiny lemon leaves of the birches.

'But Stalin hated us even more for what we had done to save the country from the Nazis, I think.

'At the beginning of the war he disappeared from view for ten days after Hitler attacked us on mid-summer night in 1941. Some people claim that Stalin had a breakdown. But I think that he was working furiously to save his skin. He sent a message to Hitler saying that he would surrender and make a separate peace and give the Germans all the territory that Lenin gave them in the peace in March 1918. Hitler was fool enough to turn down his offer, but Stalin was hedging his bets by keeping in touch with Hitler.* The link might be useful to him one day

'Then, when he made his first broadcast he called us "Brothers and Sisters". We were the people he'd

---

* How Babushka knew this, Andrei would never discover. He came to understand that, over the years, she had known the unlikeliest people and that they had entrusted to her their deepest secrets. She never gossiped and never showed off. She never gave them away. She spoke only to Andrei and he was faithful to her. Years later, Andrei read the books of authors, like Alexander Yakovlev and Dmitry Volkogonov, who had access to secret archives after the fall of the Communist Party in 1991. General Volkogonov confirmed from the archives that Stalin sought a separate peace with Hitler in June 1941, using as an inter-mediary Stemanov, the Bulgarian Ambassador in Moscow, one of his secret agents. Bulgaria was allied to Hitler at that time. In later years Stalin falsely accused Churchill and Roosevelt of seeking a separate peace with Hitler.

persecuted, but those were his first words, "Brothers and Sisters"... The words of a bully and a coward...

'Previously I had feared him, now I despised him...

'He lived in a small room, buried away in the depths of the Kremlin or in his dacha in the forest. For years he worked through the night, and slept all morning. He only used to go out and see the city at night when there was no one on the streets. He was afraid of us. He didn't trust us.

'When Hitler attacked, he couldn't believe it. Two years before that, he'd made an agreement with Hitler that they would not attack each other, and they divided Poland and the rest of Eastern Europe between them. He abandoned Great Britain and France to Hitler. The Nazis and the Bolsheviks, Hitler and Stalin, divided Poland between them.'

'That was when Britain declared war on Germany,' said Andrei. 'September 1939.'

Babushka nodded.

'I remember the shock many naïve, simple, innocent people felt when it was announced in the papers and on the radio that Stalin had made that deal with Hitler. They didn't see that Stalin would do anything. He did it to gain time. He'd destroyed all his rivals in our country. Then he realised how great Hitler's power had grown, and the only way to save himself was to share out the spoils in Europe with him.

'Some people say that Stalin had been planning to attack Hitler and conquer the whole of Europe after the Germans and the British and French wore each other out in the War. That was the real point of the agreement with Hitler. He wanted them to destroy each other so that he could take over all Europe and make use of Germany's factories.

'In their talks with him in August the British and French stupidly told Stalin that if Hitler attacked the Poles they would declare war on Germany. It meant that Stalin knew that they really intended to fulfil their threat. Hitler thought that, as usual, they were just bluffing. So Stalin made his pact with Hitler and let him attack Poland, and moved the chess pieces that started the War. Then, when Germany, Great Britain and France were destroying each other, he planned to rout them all. That was his idea. It's obvious.

'He always set out to destroy all his opponents, one by one. That's the key to Stalin. Grasp this, Andrei, and you understand everything about him.

'But Hitler sensed Stalin's preparations and made his attack first. It was suicide for the Germans... But at first Stalin thought he was finished and offered Hitler all he wanted, just like Lenin and the Kaiser in 1918. Hitler was such a fool that he ignored the offer.

'"Brothers and sisters",' Babushka laughed, 'what a hypocrite and coward he was. He thought he'd flatter us. But we didn't break down. We fought and resisted, and drove the Nazis to Berlin. But we did it *despite Stalin*. We did it for our country, not for him.

'And he knew it and he was envious. He knew that all the toadying and applause that he received were lies. In all these years I've never heard anyone praise him sincerely, in all the millions of words poured over him. And he knew it was all a sham and he feared and despised us.

'Stalin didn't regard the defeat of Hitler as a victory. He wanted all Europe. He didn't even inspect the troops at the victory parade in Moscow. He was the supreme commander of Soviet forces, but he told Marshal Zhukov to inspect them. At the banquet after the parade, he said that any people but the Russians would have hanged their leaders after the calamity that they had suffered. But we didn't hang him, so he despised us and hated us all the more, and he began to torture us again.

'He declared Leningrad a "hero city". Perhaps it was some ghastly, cynical joke, deriding us for the blockade when the top Communists got most of what little food was left in the city. Akademik Dmitry's friends told him what the Party bosses did.

'Immediately, Stalin began planning the third world war. He never gave up. He knew that Communist power had to keep expanding to the ends of the earth. The persecutions started up again. The repression at home was vital to his aims and couldn't stop.

'Then a miracle happened for me. Igor had been the Academician's pupil for a few months before the Nazis invaded. He recognised Igor's gifts, and after the war he recommended him for a post at the university in Moscow. Igor could have waited for a post in Leningrad, but I think that the Academician saw that we both needed to leave Leningrad...

'Somehow we got permission to settle in Moscow. It must have been because Igor was given the post as an assistant at the university. He had served in the forces during the blockade, and this was his reward. We settled in a tiny flat, and then he met your mother, and they moved into the bigger flat that had belonged to her parents. They asked me to live with them. This dacha and the land had belonged to your mother's parents, too.

'This garden is my miracle; this, and your parents' happiness... It has cocooned them, and they have saved me. You arrived very quickly, too, and you helped.'

Babushka smiled broadly. She looked thirty years younger.

'Now you know everything.'

'I remember the greyness and the darkness,' said Andrei. 'I remember those huge rooms in the flat when I was only three or four years old. I used to look out of the window at the Moscow river, and round to the side was the Kremlin, and opposite it the British Embassy, guarded by the police to keep out visitors.

'In that little chest that you gave me for my room was a copy of the *British Ally* newspaper, with a picture of the three War leaders. Stalin and Churchill were sitting on either side of Roosevelt. That's what made me long to learn English.

'It must have been because Mother's father was one of the first to be rehabilitated after Stalin's death that it was possible for me to go to England. That and the Academician watching over us all. I didn't understand it for years. The rehabilitation made a great difference to Mother. After that she got better work as a translator.'

'Hundreds of thousands, millions of people re-appeared,' said Babushka. 'They were reunited with their families. Some had spent ten, fifteen, even twenty-five years in the prison camps. Millions had died, probably as many of us as in the War. Twenty million died in the War because of Stalin's mistakes, and there were twenty million more deaths because of Bolshevism. Millions more in the Civil War.*

'The Party tried to exorcise Stalin's ghost, but they were still Lenin's Party, Stalin's Party. The test came in Hungary, and it showed that nothing had changed.'

'Yet something *had* changed,' said Andrei. 'The Hungarians had challenged Communism. They just wanted to throw it off, to get rid of our Army, to get rid of us all. They regarded us as an oppressor, not as a liberator. After that, the whole world knew that Communism survived there only by force of arms. Even as a child I saw it. Our leaders must have known it in their hearts. Perhaps it was the same in all those countries in Eastern Europe. And now it is the same in Czechoslovakia, although there Mr Dubcek and the others are being much more cautious than the Hungarians were.'

---

* See *Ten Leaders from Lenin to Medvedev* by D.A. Volkogonov and L.M. Mlechin (2011). General Volkogonov calculates the number of deaths as follows (p.651, Russian edition): 13 million in the Civil War; 21.5 million in the Great Terror; and 26.5 million in the Second World War – a total of 61 million.

'Whatever happens now, it cannot last for ever,' said Babushka. 'It is all built on lies and force.'

The sun was sinking as Babushka and Andrei continued their conversation. On and on they talked, all day.

It was living history, the story of a country, of a family, of Babushka's life. It was a picture of the life into which Andrei had been born, of all the forces that would shape his own life.

Proud of their day's work, they sat on the bench drinking tea, feeling the chill in the air as evening came and the small cumulus clouds carried by the north-west wind turned from silver to pink to orange to gold and red and finally dark purple. The stars began to appear. The potatoes were planted carefully and deep, well protected from the May frosts.

Andrei collected some birch logs from the wood-pile. A sweet smell emerged from the stove as he opened the door to build up the fire for the evening.

In the midst of all the tragedy of their country and family, which they had discussed all day, there was a mysterious comfort as they sat close together by the stove and let its warmth envelop them and soothe their muscles and their hearts.

Moscow

Wᴇᴇᴋ by week the movement for reform in Prague grew stronger. The press, television and radio in all countries wanted to report on the Soviet attitude to Mr Dubcek and the Prague Spring. A few Soviet diplomats became unsettled and began to question their work. The KGB reported on them and tried to stop them defecting to the West. Out of the blue, in some Western country, a Soviet diplomat or trade representative might be called home on his own 'for consultations', when he fell under suspicion. Some days later, when he had been trapped in Moscow, all his family would also be taken back.

It was such a recall from the London Embassy that gave Andrei his chance; not that Andrei was told about that.

'Because your English is the best among your group, we are sending you for eight weeks to assist as a clerk in the consular department in London,' his boss told him, sitting at the head of his impressive mahogany meeting table.

He kept Andrei standing like a schoolboy, and in fact he still looked like one.

'Make good use of your time.'
Andrei did not need to be told that.

London

ANDREI arrived in London by train, at Liverpool Street station, after a three-day journey. He was one of three officials travelling together from Moscow, through Poland, Germany, East and West, and Holland. The others were much older, and one of them was charged with keeping an eye on him. The Ministry knew everything about Andrei; otherwise he would not have been given the job.

As the train clattered through the flat Essex countryside, with its villages and towns and light industry, and approached the outer suburbs of London, Andrei's excitement grew. There was much more traffic on the roads and the train was not drawn by a steam-engine as it had been in 1956. The clothes that the three of them were wearing seemed drab. Everything here now seemed much richer, with more colour and variety. There was a strange excitement in the air.

Andrei, deep in a book, thought about the Durhams. He had no idea what had happened to Helena or Tibor in Hungary, but he realised that most Hungarians must hate Russia and Russians. He did not know what the Durham family would think of him. He did not expect to see them.

At Liverpool Street station Andrei and his companions were met by an Embassy driver with a large Mercedes. He took the other two men to join their families at a block of flats, and then drove Andrei on to a house, a sort of hostel, for short-term workers at the Embassy. The housekeeper showed Andrei to a tiny, airless room that looked out over the chimneys of central London. Andrei sat on the bed with his luggage beside him.

It was all so different from the warm, friendly welcome the Durhams had given him at their house twelve years ago.

The next day Andrei was set to work at the Consulate. He issued visas to visitors to the Soviet Union, and conducted short interviews with applicants. Sasha, his boss, a short man with a couple of gold teeth and black-framed spectacles, always smeared with dust, watched him closely. Andrei attended minutely to his work.

Most of the applicants were former Soviet citizens who had taken British nationality, often after marriage, but there were a few tourists and businessmen. For days Andrei did nothing but move between his room in the hostel and his office. He wanted to be accepted, taken for granted and ignored.

No one spoke to him about the man whose desk he had taken. It was obvious that something odd had happened. There was not a scrap of paper, no personal belongings of any sort in the desk. It had been completely stripped. The KGB had searched it and removed everything.

Each weekend Andrei walked around London; 'swinging London', it was called at that time. He melted into the crowds of tourists. To begin with, that was not easy. His hair was cut short, Soviet-style, and he wore the rather shabby suit that he used on week-days in the office. But his hair grew and he bought a cheap jacket and jeans at a street market. His sharp, fair Slavic features still drew some inquisitive looks but his English was so good that it never betrayed his nationality. He never heard Russian spoken on the streets of London.

Andrei walked everywhere. His pay was low, and he was saving his money to take back presents to Babushka and his parents. He visited St Paul's Cathedral and stood in admiration in front of the photograph of the Cathedral crowned by a halo of fire and devastation during the London Blitz in 1940. Andrei knew that in that year Stalin was sending enormous resources of metals, oil and food to Hitler. Without them there could have been no Blitz. Many of Hitler's pilots had been trained in Russia in secret flying schools set up for Germany by Stalin in the 1920s and 1930s. Andrei did not know that most British people knew nothing about this. Some British Communists knew, but they told their usual lies.

In his English classes in Moscow Andrei had wandered far from his syllabus. He had even read some of Chaucer's 'Canterbury Tales' because his teacher had inspired his enthusiasm. Andrei walked across London Bridge and visited Southwark from where the band of pilgrims had set out on their way to Canterbury. He walked back along the Thames and saw some blocks of flats that would not have been completely out of place in Moscow. But for the most part, Moscow and London had little in common. Although London was busy, the atmosphere was easy, whereas Moscow was tense and sullen.

Andrei bought a cheap transistor radio in a street market. He followed events in Czechoslovakia closely. He avoided giving his colleagues any idea that he was taking a special interest.

'Perhaps we are all doing the same thing,' he thought.

In the Embassy there were Communist Party meetings. All members of staff were nominal members, but few people took it seriously. Everyone had to attend the meetings when the Party's line on events would be repeated. No one present betrayed his personal feelings. Andrei avoided unnecessary contact with anyone in authority, especially the KGB men. This was not easy as there were so many, almost half the staff. Even at home Andrei had never been aware of them in such great numbers. He noticed that the real diplomats resented the KGB and were envious of their higher pay and better expense accounts, exasperated that they filled so many jobs.

'Why have the British been so lax and let them all come here and stay so long?' he thought. 'Don't they care about what the KGB does? If only they knew how the real diplomats would rejoice to see them expelled for spying so they could fill their places.'

Half way through his visit, in early August, Andrei heard a report on the radio of a meeting to which the Soviet leader Mr Brezhnev summoned Mr Dubcek. It seemed that a compromise had been reached that would allow the Prague Spring to continue.

That evening Andrei listened to a discussion on the radio after the ten o'clock news.

'It is a deception,' said Geza to the interviewer. 'In the West you all wish to believe in their good will. Your leaders wish to be deceived. You all forget 1956. Then the Soviet Army actually withdrew from Budapest and the Hungarians had four days' freedom. But it was just to re-group their forces. It will be the same now. They never leave.'

As usual, two Western professors, one of them English, the other American, contested Geza's views. They almost accused him of anti-Soviet propaganda, but Geza could not be moved.

Then Giori spoke. Being the youngest person in the discussion he was given the least time to express his views. 'Yes, they will return,' he said. 'I was there in 1956. I saw them return then.'

Andrei listened attentively. He recognised Giori's voice immediately as that of the reporter he heard in Moscow on the BBC's Russian service. Now he understood much more of the reasons for Giori's outlook.

'My brother was there, too. He had been in

England. It seems incredible now. He and my sister had been here on holiday. But they returned to us. Tibor and Helena returned.'

Andrei shivered.

'Tibor returned and he joined the uprising. We had those four days of freedom. Then the Soviet Army, and their allies, invaded in immense force. Tibor was killed; and our mother. Yes, if this Prague Spring continues the Soviet Union will crush it. They will not let Prague be free.'

Andrei could not sleep that night. He tossed and turned in his stuffy attic bedroom. He could not open the window. His mind raced with thoughts of the Durhams.

'Can I contact them?'

In the twelve years, there had been only the two postcards. Andrei remembered finding them. He had come back from school in the hard frost and darkness of a mid-January afternoon in Moscow and collected the post from the large wooden box in the entrance hall of their block of flats. There, together with a weekly literary paper to which his parents subscribed, *Literaturnaya Gazeta*, he found the card from England. On each occasion there had been just a short message, but the words had brought back so vividly the holiday together.

The news from Prague grew worse. After the summit between Brezhnev and Dubcek, there was a pause. Soon it was clear that Geza and Giori's forecasts would prove true. There was tension in the Soviet Embassy. The Ambassador paid a brief visit to

Moscow. Special meetings were held to keep the staff in line and monitor them.

Andrei concentrated on his work. The days were ticking past and Andrei was well into the second half of his eight-week duty in London. He was due to return to Moscow in the first week of September. After a short holiday he would then go back to work at the Ministry. He had no idea when, if ever, he would be sent back to Great Britain. He feared that the thread that linked him with the Durhams would be cut for ever.

On Wednesday, the twenty first of August, Andrei turned on his transistor radio for the seven o'clock news as he got up.

The Soviet Army had invaded Czechoslovakia overnight.

'Always overnight,' Andrei thought. 'Just like the German invasion of the Soviet Union in 1941 and our invasion of Hungary in 1956; just like Grandfather's arrest.'

Mr Dubcek's government ordered their forces to offer no resistance, and asked the general population not to fight. Within hours the Soviet Army had seized all the key points and had the country in its grip.

Dissidents were arrested and imprisoned, then deprived of the means of earning a living except by manual labour. Their courage was destined to prove more powerful than Communism. Twenty-five years later, Vaclav Havel, one of the dissidents imprisoned and persecuted by the Soviet invaders in 1968, became President of Czechoslovakia.

President Havel remembered those who had stood by the dissidents when they were persecuted and he expressed his people's thanks to them. He was amazed at the ideological criticism in Great Britain of Mrs Thatcher. Some of the critics, perhaps many of them, had been only too happy to see the Soviet Union reassert its control over Czechoslovakia in 1968. They were themselves hoping for 'Communism with a human face' in their own country. Speaking to them of Mrs Thatcher, President Havel said, 'To you she is "the Iron Lady", but to us she is dear, kind Mrs Thatcher without whose support and conviction we would still be the slaves of Soviet Communism.'

In the Soviet Embassy in late August everyone was watching everyone else. There were demonstrations outside. The police kept the demonstrators well back from the buildings.

In his office Andrei felt that one or two of his colleagues might share his shame at what their country had done. A few people did not look him in the eye. Most seemed indifferent. They had seen it all before and expected to see it again.

The Embassy was constantly busy. Apart from everything else, the staff had to deal with over a hundred musicians on a short visit from Moscow. On the very evening of the invasion the USSR Symphony Orchestra was to give a performance at the Proms at the Royal Albert Hall. The programme included the 'cello concerto of the Czech composer,

Anton Dvorak. The soloist was Mstislav Rostropovich, the greatest Russian 'cellist of the century. He and his wife, the soprano Galina Vishnevskaya, were already risking their own safety by giving refuge to Alexander Solzhenitsyn. They allowed him to write *The Gulag Archipelago*, hiding in the garden shed at their dacha. Six years later Solzhenitsyn would be deprived of his citizenship and exiled from the Soviet Union.

Rostropovich's manner that evening was unsettled. He expressed himself by reducing the music at times to a barely audible whisper. For an encore he played the slow movement of a Bach 'cello suite.

There were more Party meetings in the Embassy, warning staff of the dangers that the British or Americans might try to provoke some of them to defect and betray their Motherland.

The days passed. The West accepted that nothing could be done to save Czechoslovakia. Some sort of calm was restored.

There were only three days left before Andrei had to go back to Moscow.

On Sunday the first of September he went for a walk in Hyde Park around the Serpentine. In the middle of the morning he turned out of the park and walked to Ennismore Gardens. In the quiet street he saw the tall, Italianate tower of the building which the Church of England had given to the Russian Orthodox congregation in London for them to convert into an Orthodox Cathedral.

The Cathedral had become the centre of the small Russian community in London. Father Antony, the priest in charge, was well known by radio and television to countless people, respected by believers and atheists, bearing witness tirelessly to the power of Christ, Whom, as he told inquirers, he had met as the Risen Lord, converting him as a fifteen year old from a runaway to become believer, doctor, resistance fighter in Nazi-occupied Paris and, finally, priest.

At home Andrei never went to church. No one known to do so would have been acceptable in any Soviet organisation, let alone in the diplomatic service.

Most of the churches in Russia had been closed, tens of thousands of them. The open confession of religious belief was dangerous. In 1918 Lenin and Trotsky unleashed the greatest persecution of Christians in the world's history. Lenin chose Trotsky especially for the task because of his ruthless, efficient cruelty. His role was kept secret at the time and remained so for seventy-five years. Stalin continued the persecution, except during the War, and Khrushchev revived it in the 1950s and 1960s. Many of the Russian Orthodox bishops and priests, perhaps the Patriarch himself, were KGB agents.

In Berlin, on his 'Pioneer' holiday in 1961, Andrei had slipped away from the group for an hour and had visited a church service. He had been embarrassed by his ignorance of how to behave, when to cross himself and bow. Soon he forgot about that and he was exalted by the music and by the movement of the liturgy.

He was amazed when three Russian soldiers based in East Berlin entered the church and stood quietly, bowing their heads in prayer. When he looked again they had slipped out. Soon he also left.

The Cathedral in Ennismore Gardens was mainly used by Russians who had left their country as exiles after 1917 and by their children and grandchildren. On impulse, Andrei went to join those going in for the service. He was taking a risk. Cars travelling to and from the Soviet Embassy passed along Kensington Gore and he might be spotted. But now something forced him to do this. Perhaps it was a sense of shame for his timidity as well as for what his fellow country-men were doing in Czechoslovakia and had done in Hungary.

There were some English worshippers. The Durhams used to go up to the cathedral from time to time on a Sunday to hear Father Antony preach, first in Russian, then in English. He seemed to carry the stillness of God with him, and the family always went back home enriched by his words and presence.

'I was at a lecture he gave once,' Barbara told Margaret. 'It was a debate between Christians and atheists in a grand lecture theatre. But as Father Antony came in, so still, so straight, all of us fell silent, believers and unbelievers alike. It was the only response somehow to what he carried within him. It can only have been God Who did that'

'And think,' John added, 'All the people like him, thousands and thousands of priests and nuns and monks, all swept away and tortured and killed by Lenin and Trotsky and Stalin. It's no wonder that Russia has never recovered.'

Andrei stood by a column where an icon was hanging.

The choir chanted the service, responding to the priest who led the worship. The priest stood in the doorway set in the screen, covered in icons, which separated the nave, full of worshippers, from the sanctuary which was ablaze with candles.

A strange feeling began to steel over Andrei. It was not just the hypnotic, resonant quality of the unaccompanied chanting, nor the sharp sweetness of the incense that crept into every corner of the cathedral. Andrei could not follow much of the meaning of the chant, which was in an ancient form of Russian, Church Slavonic. But he could understand the frequent refrain '*Gospodi pomiloy,*' 'Lord have mercy', and the assurance of God's forgiveness and love. He sensed in the bearing of the congregation, especially the older men and women, something special that he had seen in Babushka and Akademik Dmitry. They represented a people which had been mercilessly exterminated, deliberately swept aside, and whose history had been replaced by the lies of Soviet propaganda. In some new way Andrei felt himself identified with his people who had endured so much.

'If only Babushka...,' he thought. 'If only she were here. If only we were together.'

Andrei tore himself away from the service and left the cathedral as the congregation was lining up to receive the bread and wine of the Holy Communion. Throughout the service people quietly came and went. No one took any notice of him.

On his way back to Hyde Park, Andrei came to the Albert Hall. There was a queue for tickets for a special concert to take place the following afternoon. Large posters at the front of the hall were advertising it, in aid of refugees from Czechoslovakia.

'If only...,' thought Andrei, and turned to walk back to his room to begin to prepare for his return to Moscow.

Although Andrei did not know it, Sasha, his boss was pleased with his work. Andrei had caused him no trouble and the Consul had praised Sasha for his careful handling of a dangerous situation. For a while the KGB had stopped harassing him.

'He's not a bad young man,' Sasha said to the Consul.

'Let him have half a day to do some shopping. He's worked well and been so mouse-like,' the Consul said. His generosity was unprecedented and never to be repeated. It showed his relief at having the KGB off his back when everyone else was unsettled because of Czechoslovakia.

Andrei could not believe his luck. Perhaps his time in the cathedral had stirred something in him that had to be expressed openly. Perhaps it was simply the sight of all the young people in the queue at the Albert Hall, so free to express their feelings that touched Andrei's heart. He went back on Monday afternoon and joined those waiting to buy tickets to stand in the arena or gallery.

'Where are you from?' asked the young woman standing next to Andrei in the queue. She was obviously a student, one of hundreds waiting to buy tickets.

'From France,' said Andrei. He hoped that he would not have to say more, but if need be he could say that his parents had emigrated from Russia to France after the Revolution. There was a big Russian community there that had kept up its traditions and continued to live a life of its own in Paris.

'Have you heard Jacqueline du Pre before?' Andrei asked the young woman who introduced herself as Mary, and her boyfriend, Robert.

'At the Proms,' Robert told him. 'She played Elgar's Cello Concerto.'

Robert and Mary told Andrei enthusiastically about the Proms. To Andrei's relief, they talked non-stop.

Soon Andrei said goodbye to them and went up to the gallery. He joined the others there leaning over the rail or sitting on the floor. Before the music started, Daniel Baremboim, the conductor and husband of Jacqueline du Pre, the soloist, spoke to the audience.

'We are not demonstrating against any state or people,' he said. 'We are simply expressing our sympathy for all those who are suffering in Czecho-slovakia.'

The main work in the concert was, again, the 'cello concerto by Dvorak. Jacqueline du Pre played it passionately, with wide, strong movements of her bow, her fair hair falling around her face and over her shoulders. It was an intense performance, and it caught the mood of the audience. At the beginning of the third movement, one of the strings in the 'cello snapped. Carried away by the atmosphere, Jacqueline du Pre burst into tears as she replaced the broken string. The performance restarted. Andrei's face, too, was wet with tears.

'It all goes back to Babushka,' Andrei thought, 'and to what she and Akademik Dmitry knew and believed in. I will not fail them.'

The passion of that incident, Andrei thought, spoke much more eloquently to the audience's feelings about the rape of Czechoslovakia than Baremboim's speech.

'How can anyone sympathise with Czechoslovakia without expressing outrage at what has been done to her, and at those who have done it?'

Baremboim must have spoken from idealistic motives, Andrei thought, but his words could only give comfort to those who had crushed the movement for freedom.

'It matters so much to our leaders that they can stifle criticism and find people abroad to speak up for their policies. If only people here knew how much it would help if they would speak openly, not in a veiled, delicate way. How much it would encourage those who wished to change things if they heard the truth openly expressed. Don't they realise that some of us hate what's been done in Czechoslovakia? Do they think that we are willing slaves?'

As the applause continued and all this was going through his mind, Andrei gazed around at the audience. Many of them were as young as him or younger: at university or in their last year at school. The two young women concentrating so hard on the music and leaning on the railing further around the gallery, for example... One of them had extraordinary black hair and pale eyes.

'They could be Helena and Margaret,' Andrei thought.

The applause ended, and the audience began to drift away. Andrei left quickly.

Andrei sat in a coffee bar, surrounded by young people from the audience. He bought a cup of coffee and flicked through the concert programme again, but he was thinking hard about the Durhams. He could not visit them. He had only forty-eight hours left in England and they lived well away from London.

Andrei took out a postcard that he had bought for the album he was making and began to write.

> I have been working in London for nearly eight weeks, but unable to visit you. Tomorrow is my last day here.
> Today at a concert I thought I saw Margaret and Helena.
> Your A.

But Andrei's heart longed for some more direct contact. On his way to the hotel he found a telephone box in a quiet street well away from the Embassy. There would be no mobile phones for twenty years.

With his back to the street, Andrei dialled the Durhams' telephone number, as he had memorised it eight years ago.

Sussex

THE telephone was ringing as John and Barbara came into the house.

They had been up to London for the day, just before the autumn term started, and had a sandwich for lunch with Giori. Margaret and Helena had met them at Charing Cross railway station after the concert at the Albert Hall.

'Giori is going to be reporting from Vienna for a while until the situation in Prague gets clearer,' John told them on the way home. 'He may be allowed a visa to go there later. There was no resistance there, just the suicide of Jan Palak.'

'A young man, hardly older than you girls, and he burnt himself to death.' Barbara shuddered. 'His name will never be forgotten, but how terrible... So cruel...'

'What is the point of resisting such invaders? Life means nothing to them. Resistance just kills more people, like Mother and Tibor.' Helena paused and added quietly, 'They learnt from us. They were right not to resist.'

'We have no idea what it is really like,' said Margaret. 'I've had such an easy life. If we had to endure here what your country has endured, Helena, or what is happening in Czechoslovakia now, or even what Andrei...'

The telephone rang persistently as they came through the door. It was from the third call box that Andrei had visited.

'Hello,' said Helena who had run on ahead of the rest. She was hoping that it was Giori, telephoning to tell her more about his move to Vienna. 'Hello,' she said again. She put down her bag and slipped off her jacket.

'This is Helena.'

'This is Andrei.'

'*Andrei...?*'

'Did I see you and Margaret at the concert?'

'How...?'

'Helena, I am so sorry... Tibor, I'm so sorry...'

'... dead, and Mother... Giori escaped with me.'

Neither of them could believe that this conversation was taking place. Andrei's heart was pounding as he looked anxiously out of the telephone box. He felt that if people from the Embassy saw him, they would immediately report him.

Helena was torn between the memories of the holiday she and Tibor and Margaret had with Andrei so long ago and the bitterness she felt towards the Russians. She had thought the bitterness had gone,

but now it clutched her heart. But then she remembered Andrei, so shy, vulnerable, swimming, running
across the beach. Silenced by her mixed feelings, she
passed the telephone to John.

'Andrei?'

'Mr Durham, I have been working in London...'

'Where?'

'... I could not leave England without contacting
you...'

'Can we...?'

'... I don't know if I shall ever return to England.
It all depends on my work...'

'We often talk about you and that holiday.'

'... We are not all monsters, Mr Durham...'

'We *know* you, Andrei. We shall not forget you;
none of us will.'

'I do not forget any of you.'

'We often think of you, Andrei. For ever and
ever...'

'For ever and ever... Forgive me for Tibor.'

The line died. Andrei's money had run out. He leant
against the side of the narrow, red telephone box,
holding the receiver up to his ear. There was someone
waiting, impatiently, outside, looking at his watch and
trying to catch Andrei's eye. But Andrei continued to
hold the telephone to his ear for a while as he fought
to control the sobs in his chest. He stepped out onto
the street, and turned away to walk by a roundabout
route to his flat. It was cooler now, and Andrei sat on
a bench quietly for a while and then went home to
begin his packing.

John, too, held the telephone after the line went dead. He did not want to put it back on the rest, as if that would for ever cut the link with Andrei. He had his left arm around Helena's shoulder.

'Working in London,' he said.

'He must be a diplomat, I suppose,' said Margaret. She had sent off for the application forms for the British Foreign Office a few weeks ago and had not yet decided whether to apply.

'He is lucky to get to London so soon,' said Helena.

'A short visit, I suppose,' said John. 'They must be in chaos because of Czechoslovakia.'

They talked about the telephone call all that evening, and about Tibor and Helena's mother, and tried to guess what Andrei was doing in London.

'Andrei took a risk, you know,' said John.

'He won't survive in that system,' said Barbara.

'Crushed,' said Margaret.

'If he's a diplomat, he'll have to speak up for what his country does,' said Helena. 'He'll come to hate himself for doing it.'

'Giori said it's like acting in a play in Hungary now,' said John. 'They are all speaking their lines, because those are the lines the author has written for them. They behave in the way the director of the play makes them behave, but no one believes in it. Even the Communist Party and the secret police know that it isn't real.'

'Lies and force,' said Margaret.

'It pays the bosses,' said Helena. 'They take their orders from Moscow, but it's all pretence. Even in Moscow they must know that it's all pretence. They must know that we hate them and would desert them if we had a chance.'

'Your uprising achieved a lot,' said Barbara, 'but the cost was terrible.'

'Yes, we achieved a lot,' said Helena. 'They know that we hate them, that we want them to go, all of them, our own Communists and the Soviet Army and the Warsaw Pact armies. They know that no one would join that side willingly, whatever the faults there may be here in the West.'

'Even the invasion of Czechoslovakia is a victory,' said Margaret. 'They were right not to resist. It all shows that it is built on lies and force, that no one wants it.'

'But how will we ever get rid of it?' said Helena.

'Will you join the Foreign Office?' Barbara asked Margaret. They went into the kitchen, leaving the others to their discussion and began to prepare supper.

'I think so. All these events this year; imagine being part of that, witnessing things like this and living abroad... It would be such an interesting life. Growing up with Helena and Giori, it's helped me see our country as others see it, and to know how much we have to give to the world.'

'Dad and I would be so proud of you.'

At supper Helena said, 'I try to remember what our life was like before we came here, but it gets more and more difficult. Giori and I owe you so much.'

'You have given us more than we have given you,' said Barbara.

'You are our family,' said John.

'We've seen everything in a different, deeper way because of you and Giori,' said Margaret.

'I keep trying to imagine what it has been like for Andrei,' said Helena. 'It was brave of him to speak to me like that.'

'I remember that holiday so well, every moment of it,' said Barbara. 'You and Tibor were so much more like Margaret. You were so much less nervous and controlled than he was. He seemed driven, always tense, as if something terrible might happen to him at any moment.'

'A lot will depend on his friends,' said John. 'If only he had friends like...'

John was holding the photograph that he always kept in his wallet of Margaret, Helena, Tibor and Andrei, taken at the end of the holiday on the beach after their last swim. The photograph was faded and a little worn.

'Like Helena and Margaret...,' he went on, looking down at the photo. It had been a false dawn.

'And like *Tibor*,' Margaret added firmly. 'If only Tibor...'

'But there will be no one,' said Helena. 'There will be no one he can trust in their diplomatic service and embassies, no one. Just rivals, not friends; and agents of the KGB, all of them watching for any free thought or unguarded word. He will have to conform to their ways. He will explode under the strain of it all. No friends, no one to trust...'

London

TUESDAY was Andrei's last full day in London. Sasha was still glowing from the Consul's praise. He took Andrei to have a drink in a pub near the Embassy.

'Not a bad young man,' Sasha said to himself again. 'So quiet, but at least he won't cause us any problems.'

Apart from this visit to the pub, Andrei had had no social contact with him during his eight weeks in London. He had none at all with any British people apart from handling their visa papers and in the queue for the concert.

On Wednesday morning Andrei closed the door of his tiny bedroom for the last time. He was to return to Moscow by air. One of the Embassy's chauffeurs had to visit Heathrow to collect a senior diplomat returning from Moscow. Andrei went in the car to the airport.

People were bustling about, checking in for their flights, businessmen, holiday makers, young and old, casually dressed. Everywhere there was a buzz of excitement. Andrei soaked it all in as he made his way to the gate for his flight. He might well not come this way again, and he knew it. Suddenly the atmosphere changed. As people came near the gate for the plane going to Moscow, everyone – foreigners and Russians – somehow became more controlled, subdued and apprehensive. It just happened. People looked furtively at each other for a moment and turned away.

Andrei knew all too well what he was going back to. On the aircraft he settled down to read a copy of *Pravda*. He concentrated on it, his eyes screwed up and tense, as he tried to blot out all the impressions of the last eight weeks. He pushed them all down inside him, as he sank deeper and deeper into his sagging seat. It would make it easier for him when he got home.

MOSCOW

BY the time Andrei was in the terminal building at Moscow airport, battered and shabby, with dim, grey lighting, he had divided his mind into two. With one side he must now control all his behaviour, as if he really believed all that he had read in *Pravda* and *Izvestia* about the Soviet aims in Czechoslovakia and the 'welcome' the Warsaw Pact troops had received from the local population. This side now asserted itself; it was soaked deeply in Soviet ways and it could interpret everything it saw on the faces of the people whom Andrei met. It noticed the slightly raised eyebrows and quizzical look of the passport control officer with the bright red star on his cap as Andrei went through the special channel for those travelling on official or diplomatic passports. 'How could you enjoy this privilege of visiting the West when you are so young?' his look asked. 'Who is your father? A member of the Communist Party Nomenklatura or the KGB?'

And then there was the other side of his mind. Here Andrei held his memories of what he had learnt in London, all he had read in the special library at the Institute before he joined the Ministry, his holiday with the Durhams. There, too, were his memory of Akademik Dmitry, his conversations with Babushka who gave him access to the past of his country, a terrible past, but also to the hopes of freedom and prosperity which so many had felt until they were extinguished by the First World War and the Bolsheviks' seizure of power.

Everything on this second side of his mind Andrei had to control and hide. Over the next twenty years the strain of his unrelenting self-control at work would tell on him and his health. But he knew that a few others were in the same position, hiding from him what he hid from them. And this conviction gave him hope that one day he and all those who felt like him would recognise each other and throw off the Great Lie of the Communists and rise against it and destroy it. And then those who had the power in the state, and the guns, would hesitate to use them. Perhaps even they would become sick of the waste of it all, the cruelty, the pretence, and would set it all aside.

Three weeks had passed since Andrei had returned from London.

'I do not know the answer,' said Babushka. 'Perhaps it is in our genes.'

'We seem to be unable to do anything in moderation.'

'The Academician told me that in England they do everything in moderation. "Nothing in excess"... He said that might be the motto of the Delphic oracle but it was the English, not the Greeks, who had really lived up to it. He longed to go there but never got the chance. "The English Lion is wise," he used to say. "It never gives up hope and is never to be defeated. May it always roar in times of danger".'

It was late September. Andrei and Babushka were harvesting the crops at the dacha: potatoes and onions to store, and cabbage and beetroot which Babushka would pickle and bottle for the winter.

'It makes them difficult to get to know,' said Andrei. 'You can see it in the underground trains in London. There is always a little space around each person, on his own, in control of his own separate fate, not like the mass of bodies in the metro in Moscow.'

'We're so impetuous. We either love people or we hate them. Our reactions are so quick and so extreme. Perhaps that's why we've had our political history.'

'The English temperament is so mild,' said Andrei. 'Nowadays they don't need force to control each other in the way we Russians seem to need order imposed on us. The police have no guns. Imagine that.'

'Some of us have a gentleness in our souls, too,' said Babushka with a smile. 'Perhaps we would have been more like that if we hadn't suffered under the Mongol invaders for so long. They reached *Rus* and swamped us. They burnt Kiev in 1240. It was already a great European city. It had an educated population; most people there were able to read. The Mongols changed our nature for ever. They killed our leaders and took our best women as wives and bred their cruelty into some of us, alongside the kindliness and gentleness. Lenin was one of their type.

'Akademik Dmitry told me that if you wanted to see what Russia, *Rus*, might have been, you had to go to the far North West of Russia, to Karelia. The Mongols never got there and our old spirit of freedom survived. That's why he and your grandfather loved the North so much.'

'In Great Britain the monarchy is strong and the Queen very popular,' said Andrei. 'If they honour and protect their Royal family, perhaps that will give them a unity, even with all the changes happening there now.'

'Do they know what a treasure they have?' asked Babushka. 'As soon as Lenin and the Bolsheviks murdered the Tsar and his family in 1918, we were finished. There was nothing left to unite all those trying to fight the Bolsheviks...

'May God save their Queen and her family from that fate. The Bolsheviks were an alien horde. They had nothing in common with us ordinary Russians who love our country.'

Andrei made the most of every chance to leave Moscow on Saturday and spend the weekend with Babushka in the country. He caught the first electric train of the day and in an hour he was in the depths of the forest. He walked from the local station through the woods and passed Ilya's parents' grand dacha. Ilya was never there now. Andrei did not know what work he was doing, and did not risk asking his parents.

In the weeks since his return from London Andrei had seen the leaves on the silver birch trees turn yellow, then gold. The sun was still warm, an Indian Summer, in Russia called 'grandmother's summer', when Babushka and millions like her harvested their crops, preserved mushrooms for the winter and made jam for the store cupboard.

Soon there would be the first frost. The leaves would fall quickly. It would be time to close up the dacha for another year. Babushka would return to the flat in Moscow.

As she grew older she wanted to spend more and more time at the dacha. She had started to attend a small church in the village a couple of miles away. She kept herself to herself and no one there knew who she was. She discovered that some teachers, writers and doctors from Moscow came to the church on Sundays. They came to hear Father Aleksander's sermons and to discuss the Christian faith with him. Most of them were inquirers, seeking a faith to make sense of their lives. They found in Father Aleksander a sympathetic listener as well as a teacher. Babushka knew that there were bound to be KGB agents among the visitors, but for some reason she felt sure that Father Aleksander was genuine. She knew that the KGB would be more interested in the young visitors than in an old lady living in a simple dacha in the woods. She could do Andrei no harm by going to church if she kept herself anonymous.

'It is a different Russia in church,' said Babushka, 'Without the destruction brought by the Bolsheviks. It's like what I remember as a girl.'

Andrei told her about the service in the Cathedral in London.

They were sorting the potatoes into sacks, picking out those that seemed firmest and healthiest to be stored for the long winter.

'It's as if this church and its people have been purified by all the terrible years. The congregation is welcoming, not fanatics, not anti-Semitic, just Russian Christians. Father Aleksander is from a half Jewish, half Christian family. There is no nationalistic pride, yet everything seems more truly Russian than anything I've encountered since I was a young woman before 1917.'

'Do you remember what the Academician said about nationalism and patriotism?' said Andrei.

'Yes, of course. Patriotism is to love my own country and to understand that others love theirs. Nationalism is just to hate other countries and peoples.'

'We have those two forces at work in us,' said Andrei. 'A dark force of destruction that is easily unleashed, on us and on others. It is why all our neighbours in Europe hate us and fear us. Some people here like to think that they respect us, but that is not respect; it is just loathing. They know all about Stalin and Lenin before him, and Khrushchev and Brezhnev after him...

'And then there is the other side of our souls, a force of light, generous and hospitable, playful and patient.

But so often that second side is submerged in the blackness and cruelty. It is the second side that is our only hope.'

'What do they think about us in Great Britain?'

'The best people there do hate what we have done to our country and to Eastern Europe. They will never let it happen to them. Their worst people fawn on us because we are a nuclear power and a threat. There are quite a lot of their MPs and journalists and union leaders like that. They would be Quislings, just like Hitler's supporters abroad in the War.

'There are just a few people there who know enough to see that we have a good side, a different side, and that if that side were in control again, we would be a different country.'

Late on Saturday evening Babushka took Andrei to see the church. The building was open for those who wished to go there and pray. When Babushka and Andrei visited it, tired by their work in the garden, there was only one person inside, an elderly lady, cleaning the church in preparation for Sunday's service. She gave them a deep bow, and Babushka and Andrei bowed to her in reply.

The church was a white, stone building, small and squat but with a dome and a bell tower. The dome may have been golden many years ago, but now it was painted a dark blue. The bell tower had somehow survived the years. Lenin's men, many of them convicts given drugs and alcohol to stir them to madness, toppled thousands of such towers after the Revo lution, as around them the villagers had wept, unable to stop the sacrilege.

Inside the church there was an earth floor and an icon screen with a few simple icons, some of them modern, and others which had survived the Bolsheviks' looting of church treasures in the early 1920s. Lenin claimed that the treasures would be used to feed the starving population. In fact, most of the money was sent to support Communist parties abroad as they tried to foment revolution on Bolshevik orders.

Babushka stood in silence before an icon. Andrei walked around the church and soaked in the atmosphere and then went to stand beside her. The icon was a representation of the Holy Trinity, based on the story in the book of Genesis of three angels who visited Abraham at the oak trees of Mamre.

'I saw the original of that icon in the Tretyakov gallery in Moscow,' Andrei said. They were walking back to the dacha. 'It used to be at the St Sergey Monastery near Moscow.'

'It shows everything about Russia,' said Babushka. 'Andrei Rublyov was our first great icon painter. It was a time of terrible torment for our people when he painted the Trinity icon. The Mongolian Tartars had enslaved us and extorted tribute from us, and after more than a hundred years under the Mongol yoke, St Andrei painted that picture, full of colour and harmony and joy and peace.'

'It's no wonder that the world despairs of understanding us,' said Andrei.

Then and Now
Sussex, 1969

MARGARET decided not to apply for the Foreign Office. She had met a lot of diplomats over the years.

'We need them,' she thought. 'But how can they bear living in that false world?'

Her father had told her about the massacre of Polish leaders and Army officers in the Katyn Forest in the west of Russia at the start of the Second World War. The wickedness of it all had a big impact on her.

'Over twenty thousand of them were shot by Stalin's henchmen early in 1940,' John explained. 'But because Hitler attacked Russia and the Soviet Union became our ally, the British government and the Americans pretended that all those murders had been Hitler's work. It was stupid as well as wicked. How could anyone keep Stalin sweet by toadying to him? It just showed him that we *feared* him and made him despise us all the more.

'Then we didn't let the Polish forces take part in our parade in London to celebrate the victory in June 1946. The Poles had fought and died shoulder to shoulder with us for so long, only to have their country overrun by Stalin. We were exhausted as a country and so much in awe of Stalin's power... It would have been better not to have a parade.'

'You were right, Dad,' Margaret said. 'Hitler and the Nazis did win the War in the shape of Stalin and the Communists, and they have never stopped trying to defeat us.'

'For over forty years all our governments told that lie about Katyn although they knew the truth,' John added. 'It was the diplomats who had to do the lying to keep their jobs...'

'Even with us – let alone the Soviet Union – there is so much falsehood,' Margaret thought. 'What our diplomats do and say isn't always even in our own interests but they have to do it to appease foreign dictators who have too much power already.'

Years later, when President Yeltsin left office, Putin took over as president and began to move Russia back to dictatorship, concealed in bogus elections, time after time.

'What else could you expect from someone like him who had made a career in the KGB?' John asked.

He was thinking about what had happened in Russia and reminded Margaret about Katyn.

'All the Soviet leaders, even Gorbachev, denied that Stalin and Hitler had agreed a secret pact to dismember Poland and the rest of Eastern Europe. They all lied about Katyn and demanded that the Western leaders should do the same.'

Margaret recalled Solzhenitsyn's charge, so dramatic in Russian, *'Zhivee nye po lzhee'*, 'Live not according to The Lie'. Her father had quoted those words so often over the years, proof that truth and goodness had to be fought for time and again, and that victory was never certain.

'For all President Yeltsin's weaknesses,' John smiled, 'he was the opposite of a diplomat. Thank God for him. Let's always remember that it was *he* who finally swept away so many of the lies.'

'Mr Bukovsky helped him.'

'Yes. It was almost a miracle that President Yeltsin turned to him to be a witness in court to all the crimes committed by the Communists.'

'Twelve years in the GULAG,' said Margaret. 'Tortured and drugged, and then expelled from the Soviet Union, just like Solzhenitsyn, when he was only thirty-four years old... How could anyone be a better witness?'

'It was so unexpected,' said John. 'No one could have predicted that President Yeltsin would give him the authority to read all those secret Communist documents from the Party's headquarters, and now he has put them all on the internet for us to read. He even found the paper signed by Gorbachev in 1984 proving that he personally authorised sending money to Arthur Scargill when he was using the miners' strike for his own political ends. Yet Gorbachev looked Mrs Thatcher in the eye and promised her that he had not done it, a straight lie*... How pleased President Yeltsin would be that the truth is in the open now.'

* See Vladimir Bukovsky, *Moscovsky Protses* (*Moscow Trial*), 1996, Part 2, page 165.

'President Reagan was right about Gorbachev,' said Geza. ' "He's just a Communist," that's what he said about him after he met him the first time. "Never trust one".'

'Mr Bukovsky says that it was in the early 1980s that we came nearest to losing the Cold War,' said John. 'His documents show that the German Social Democratic Party and the Russians had been plotting that together since 1969...'*

'...within months of the Soviet invasion of Czechoslovakia,' said Giori.

'What they wanted was to restore the Soviet Union's reputation, and then get the Americans out of Europe and destroy NATO,' John added. 'It was only because the Soviet Union was stupid enough to invade Afghanistan in 1979 and then threaten Poland the following year that we all woke up to what the danger was, and that killed off the anti-American movement.'

'It's a scandal that he can't get his book about it all published in English,' said Margaret.

'There are just too many vested interests here; politicians and journalists who trimmed their sails to please the Communists in case they won,' said Geza. 'They want it all forgotten and will do everything they can to hide the truth.'

'Lenin and Stalin really knew the value of useful idiots like them,' said Giori. 'I've just read Lenin's last speech in 1922, kept secret for seventy-seven years...'

---

* See *Moskovsky Protses* (*Moscow Trial*), 1996, Part 1, page 4, and Part 2, pages 5ff, and elsewhere.

'*Molodyets*,'* Geza interrupted. 'You'll never change, I'm glad to say...'

'... He was explaining his policies to a meeting of Bolsheviks in the Bolshoi Theatre in Moscow, his foreign and economic policies, everything. Yet the Communists kept that speech secret for all those years. Why?'

'I dare say you'll tell us,' said Geza.

'... Because he told the truth about the Bolshevik *coup d'etat* bluntly. In the last paragraph of his very last speech he made a sort of final confession, fourteen months before he died. "We were just a tiny insignificant cell of people calling ourselves a Party, the Bolsheviks... an insignificant seed among the mass of workers in Russia, we set ourselves the task and changed everything..."'†

'*Molodyets* again,' said Geza. 'It was no revolution, just a conspiracy against Russia, a violent, military *coup d'etat* that stole Russia from the Russians. It finished the country.'

'Just think how much we owe the Poles,' said Margaret. 'They saved us at the gates of Warsaw. Heaven knows what would have happened to us all if they hadn't won when the Red Army marched on Warsaw in 1920 and if the Bolsheviks had seized power in Poland. If the Poles hadn't won that battle Communist terror could have spread across all Europe.'

* 'Good lad' (Russian).
† V.I. Lenin, *Neizvestnie Dokumenty* (*Unknown Documents*), Moscow, 1999, page 572.

178

'It's so difficult to find the truth and help people to understand,' said Giori. 'So many people want to stop us. Nowadays even the BBC is reluctant to tell some truths that it finds inconvenient. It's changing. I loved it so much, but now I fear for its future. It's so obsessed by fashion. If it loses its good name, it's gone for ever. They need to remind themselves of the difference between good and bad, and true and false. Sometimes I feel that simple words like that embarrass them now.'

'I'm grateful that the BBC still told the truth in the Cold War when I was working there with you,' said Geza. 'We have it on the best authority that "the truth shall make you free".'

'And that "The Lord, the God of Israel, is the God of truth",' said John.

Geza was thoughtful. 'Yes, it's truth that matters; not fashion and political correctness which just enslave us.'

'Perhaps it was the Cold War that somehow kept us all on the straight and narrow,' John replied.

' "Wide is the gate and broad is the way that leadeth to destruction and many there be which go in thereat, because strait is the gate and narrow is the way which leadeth unto life and few there be that find it." '

'*Molodyets,*' said Giori, smiling at Geza. 'You'll never change, either.'

'Thank God that you and Barbara saved Helena and Giori,' said Geza quietly to John.

John sank into his chair. He and Geza fell silent.

Sussex and London, 1974

MARGARET became a language teacher. Five years later, in 1974, she married Adam, Geza's son and Giori's closest friend.

There were three weddings, one in the synagogue where Geza and Miriam his wife worshipped, one in a church where all the Durhams had attended services for years and John was churchwarden, and one in a registry office in central London for all their atheist and agnostic friends in the press and media.

'No one must feel left out,' said Geza. And at the door of the registry office, where no mention of religion was permitted in the ceremony, as he greeted all their friends, he quoted with delight the words of Jesus: 'Go therefore into highways, and as many as ye find, bid to the marriage.' The atheists and agnostics, as usual, were taken aback by Geza's extraordinary mind and faith. The Christians and Jews quietly smiled; they knew how much they had in common; Geza and John were the proof of that.

Sussex and Hungary, 1985-1991

WHEN Grandfather John retired in 1989, Margaret and Adam's children, Stephen and Elizabeth, were fourteen and twelve. Grandmother Barbara died that year, a month after he retired. It happened out of the blue, an unexpected stroke that took her in a moment. John and Barbara had been married for forty-four years.

The loss knocked the heart out of John. Geza and Miriam did everything they could to help him. Talking with Geza was now John's greatest pleasure. They often talked about the days in 1956, of Hungary and Suez.

'It was a tragedy that they coincided,' said Geza. 'President Eisenhower made such a terrible mistake in opposing Eden.'

'But Eden should have explained it all better to him,' John replied. 'He saw the truth so clearly but somehow his mind was already failing and he got involved in a stupid conspiracy with France and Israel.'

'It lay heavily on Eisenhower's conscience afterwards,' Geza said. 'He wanted to set the record straight before he died.'

Eisenhower had soon regretted his policy over Suez. He confessed it was the greatest error of his life. He traced from it the many disasters which befell the World in the period after 1956. Freed from fear of the consequences, all manner of despots seized control of the countries in North Africa, the Middle East and elsewhere, so corrupting their societies. They were invariably supported by Soviet money and weapons.

'I saw the terrible consequences there when the Soviet Union sent me to Africa to teach at the university,' Geza added.

It was the beginning of a Soviet expansion and aggressive policy that continued in Africa, Asia and Europe until the 1980s, long after Eisenhower's death.

'It was a dreadful mistake, but Eisenhower was a brave man,' John said. 'He took responsibility for his actions and owned up to his failures. He was like that. In June 1944 when everyone was worried about bad weather, he took the final decision to launch the Allied invasion of Normandy on D-Day. He was completely alone and no one else could do it, and he wrote, "It is my decision. If it goes wrong, it was my decision."'

John continued to live, in a flat, in the house in Battle where he and Barbara had brought up Margaret, Giori and Helena and had had so many happy years together. Margaret and Adam now filled the rest of the big house with their family. It worked well and kept John young.

Helena had never married.

Although they did not speak the language, Stephen and Elizabeth were proud to be half-Hungarian. At first this puzzled Adam. He wished to put behind him the troubled past of his father's country and be 'nothing but British', as he put it. It was through Stephen and Elizabeth's interest that Adam was reconciled to his roots.

The two of them became inquisitive about Andrei, who so long ago, for such a short, intense time, had been friends with Mother and Aunt Helena and Uncle Tibor, later to die a hero's death.

'What can have happened to Andrei, Mum?'

'Will we ever meet him, Dad?'

Occasionally a postcard would arrive from Andrei, addressed to their grandfather, from some distant country, but never from Russia itself. The only explanation was that he was serving his country abroad. The postcards became a little more frequent after Stephen's tenth birthday in 1985 when Gorbachev came to power in the Soviet Union and contacts with the West increased.

'Perhaps Andrei will just appear here one day, Granddad,' they wondered.

But Andrei's work never brought him to Britain again. John and Barbara never visited Russia.

'Not until the country is free,' said John. They expected never to see that day.

Helena worked for the British Council promoting British arts and culture and the English language and literature. She served in many countries in Europe. In 1988 she was offered a job in Budapest.

She had not visited Hungary since 1956. She spoke the language occasionally to please John when they were together. She thought hard before accepting the posting. Finally, she did so. It had become necessary for her, too, to come to terms with the past.

Stephen and Elizabeth were excited that Helena was going to work in 'our second country'. A year later Margaret and Adam took them there for two weeks' holiday in July. They stayed with Helena in the smart flat that the Council rented for her and together they visited many parts of the country. They swam in Lake Balaton. As they all drove back to Budapest, Helena told them again the story of her flight from Hungary, thirty-three years ago, with Giori. The road was now a fast, impressive highway. Everywhere the villages and small towns had been developed and the people seemed quite well off.

Despite all the changes Helena was not reconciled to what had happened. She could not feel that this had once been her home. She did not know where Mother and Tibor were buried. Real freedom was not possible as long as the Communists held power and the Soviet Army occupied garrisons throughout the country.

That autumn Gorbachev loosened the Soviet Union's grip on Eastern Europe. He made it clear that the Soviet Army would not again invade those countries in order to keep their Communist Parties in power. They must reform like Russia. He expected them to do so and to hold on to government. A Soviet wit called it the Frank Sinatra doctrine, 'You can do Communism your way, and "I'll do it my way".'

At the first free elections for over forty years Hungary rejected the Communist Party. Country after country went the same way. Gorbachev and the Soviet leaders were shocked by the results. They had not realised how much the peoples of Eastern Europe hated them and their system. As soon as they had the chance, they seized it and threw out the Communists. The whole thing was unplanned, a mistake, an accident, made real only by the desire of the peoples everywhere behind the Iron Curtain to be free.

Over the next two years Soviet troops were withdrawn from one country after another. They returned to their homeland which did not have adequate barracks to house them. Gorbachev had intended nothing like this.

In November 1989 Germans in East and West Berlin began to take down the Berlin Wall, brick by brick. West and East Germany were soon to be reunited.

Despite the euphoria Helena held back from returning to its rest in Hungary's earth the handful of her soil that Giori had scooped up. She kept it in a little box in a drawer in her desk.

'Not yet,' she thought.

There were still Soviet troops in Hungary.

MOSCOW,
1989-1991

ANDREI visited Babushka at the dacha whenever he was at home in Moscow in the summer. Their time together was running out.

In 1989, over the May Day holiday, the two of them were working together on the vegetable plot, a ritual they loved.

'I have been lucky,' said Babushka. 'I have lived to see the start of a great change. I remember the despair that gripped my family as the First World War and the Bolsheviks destroyed us. The despair never lifted. Now there seems to be some hope.'

Andrei, too, felt that he had been lucky. His work in the Ministry had been full of interest. Except for his time in London at the start of his career, he had been sent to small countries to work in embassies and consulates, places insignificant in the Cold War. The KGB had less work to do in such places. That was how he was never pressurised by them to help them in their operations.

His competitive and careerist colleagues tried to avoid the postings that he wanted. They were keen to work in Western Europe or North America. That was the last thing that Andrei wanted. He went out of his way to make himself invisible and insignificant. He deliberately concentrated on abstruse, academic matters and revealed none of his deep knowledge and thought about big, contentious issues.

'How can he have become so dull, such a pedant?' his bosses thought. 'As a young man he seemed so brilliant.' But they were happy because unlike some others he never caused them any trouble.

Andrei shared his true views only with Babushka. It was their hidden life. No one else had an inkling of it. He had no wife, no children, but while Babushka was alive he was not lonely.

'I felt some of that hope for the first time last year,' said Andrei. 'During the special conference of the Communist Party some of the delegates began to speak the truth.'

'Everyone here watched it on television,' said Babushka. 'It was like a new beginning... *Truth* on television! I stayed up every night to watch it. We all did. And now lots of the worst Communists have been defeated at the first free elections for the Supreme Soviet.'

Babushka, born in the first year of the twentieth century, was still in good health and able to spend the summer at the dacha. Andrei's father and mother had moved back to Leningrad fifteen years ago. The Academician had arranged for Igor to take over his post there. Babushka stayed on in their Moscow flat, and Andrei lived there with her when he was not serving abroad. In winter, the two of them went to concerts and galleries together.

'But they are still killing people to stay in power,' said Babushka. 'Twenty or thirty people were shot in a demonstration in Georgia last month.'

'In the West they are debating whether Gorbachev authorised the killings,' said Andrei.

'As if the Generals would dare to order that sort of thing without his signature on a piece of paper,' said Babushka. 'They have no idea in the West how things work here.'

'Anyway, they don't realise that that is irrelevant,' said Andrei. 'If he authorised it, it is bad. But if he didn't, that is bad too. It would mean that they can commit such acts without bothering to consult him. It means that the worst sort will hold on to power to the bitter end.'

'And which side will win if it comes to violence? Babushka asked. 'No one can say.'

A sudden shower of hail, from a single black cloud in a blue sky, pounded the vegetable plot. Babushka and Andrei retreated under cover and warmed themselves by the stove.

At the end of September the following year, 1990, Babushka and Andrei spent the last weekend of the year together at the dacha. The leaves were still golden but they were falling in drifts in the still bright air, as the sun melted the hoar frost.

On Sunday they attended the service at the church.

The congregation had grown. Two months earlier Father Aleksander had been murdered as he made his way to church. Everyone knew it was the work of the KGB, the sort of crime that was never solved.

The congregation was deeply shocked, much more than they would have been a few years earlier. Then, the KGB would have acted sooner to snuff out Father Aleksander. They could not allow truth and goodness to begin to flourish. Any truth, any goodness just showed up the Soviet system for what it was.

It was Father Aleksander's death that caused Andrei, for the first time, openly to attend the church services that autumn with Babushka. He was clear in his own mind on which side he stood. There was a sense among the worshippers that, like Father Aleksander, they were fighting in a battle between good and evil, truth and lies, and they were confident that, in God's mercy, good must finally triumph.

A month later Andrei found Babushka dead in their flat in Moscow when he came home from work. She was lying in front of the icon in the corner of the dining room, clutching a tiny cross in her right hand. Her funeral service at the church near the dacha was attended by most of the congregation and she was buried there.

Igor and Natasha mourned her loss, but Andrei's grief was much deeper. Babushka, forty-five years older than him, had been his best friend for so long. He was now alone.

Soon Gorbachev had to make a fateful choice. He chose the old Communist way. By the end of that year those of his old colleagues who had worked hardest for deep political and constitutional reforms were ignored or rejected, or in despair decided to resign. On Gorbachev's orders the KGB subjected them to surveillance and harassment.

In January 1991, when the local population was trying to assert its independence in Lithuania, the most westerly republic of the Soviet Union, Soviet troops killed thirty or more civilians during a demonstration. Great Britain and the other Western countries had never accepted that Lithuania and the other states on the Baltic Sea, Latvia and Estonia, were legally part of the Soviet Union because Stalin seized them in 1940 after he and Hitler dismembered Eastern Europe together.

Geza's old question, 'Are they willing to kill their people to stay in power?' was still receiving the same answer.

The killings in Lithuania galvanised the supporters of reform. Hundreds of thousands of people of all sorts demonstrated in Moscow. It seemed that they might have their way. Gorbachev and the Communist hierarchy and the KGB were stunned for a while, but then they set about making plans to restore their full power.

Hungary, Moscow
and Sussex,
1991

TWO months later Andrei was sent to the Soviet
Embassy in Budapest as a temporary cultural attaché.
Totally reliable but never given much promotion, he
was regarded as one of the few diplomats who could
take on any task at short notice.

Andrei felt reluctant to go to work in Budapest,
which he had never visited. The vivid memories of
Helena and Tibor and of their holiday together in
England so long ago troubled him. Of course, he had
no choice about the posting.

In the early summer of 1991 Andrei caught sight
of Helena at a diplomatic reception. He had been
thinking of her and Tibor so much that he recognised
her almost immediately at the far end of the garden
where the party was being held. He left quickly. His
hands were shaking as he started his car to go home
to his flat. Later, he learnt from someone that she was

working at the British Council offices and that she was due to return to England for good in the autumn.

Helena gave no sign of noticing him in the crush at that reception but she had recognised him, too, and took the precaution of checking his name. Then she waited.

In August they had a short talk as they were leaving another diplomatic reception. They arranged to meet the following Sunday, high in the old city of Buda, overlooking the Danube and Pest, the city on the plain.

Leaning on the stone wall not far from the cathedral on the hill above the Danube, Helena and Andrei looked down over the city. The sky was darkening and the first stars appearing. On only one of the countless roof-tops in the city below them was there a neon advertising sign.

Behind them an orchestra in the courtyard played waltzes and gypsy music for the tourists eating in the restaurant built into the wall. Occasionally an accordionist performed a solo. Further away a blind man serenaded passers by on his violin; a battered wooden box stood on the cobbles in front of him to collect money.

To their left, across the Danube, Helena and Andrei saw a building, strangely like and unlike the Parliament building at Westminster. To their right, a bridge stretched its chain link curves over the river, rather like the bridge over the Thames at Hammersmith.

Helena's family had lived beside this river for two hundred years until she had been forced to flee by the Soviet invasion. The columns of tanks had been driven mostly by Russians like him, Andrei kept thinking.

It was midnight when Andrei and Helena turned away from the view of the River Danube and the city. There had been so much to talk about and to explain, so many difficult questions and answers. There had been bitterness and anger, but later a new hope. They lived again the time at Woody Bay with John and Barbara, Margaret and Tibor. The intense memory of Tibor and the story of his death gave their hope a strange strength.

'He didn't want violence,' said Helena.

'He just wanted freedom. The violence was forced on him, and by the Communists who enslaved my people, too.' Andrei could hardly control his feelings.

They walked through the streets stretching along the crest of the hill of Buda, which were almost deserted by now. The funicular cable car which carried passengers up and down the rocky hillside all day had long ago ceased its work.

Andrei and Helena zigzagged down the footpath to the bridge over the Danube and crossed it. Even the gypsies from Rumania and the traders from Russia selling chess sets had left.

They turned and gazed at the hill, the cathedral and the battlements where they had eaten in the restaurant a few hours ago. Looking down they saw it all, and the stars, reflected in the Danube.

Next day, Monday the nineteenth of August, the world was told that hard-line Communists and the KGB had taken Gorbachev hostage at his palace in the Crimea and cut him off from Moscow and the machinery of government. It seemed to be an attempt either to seize power or to force him to come out on their side and to snuff out the freedoms that he had allowed to develop.

It later became clear that Gorbachev had been in some sort of contact with the leading plotters during his captivity. It was not possible to know for sure whether he had been acting with them in a massive pretence. Whatever the truth of that, it was too late for him and the plotters, because after seventy-five years of Communist dictatorship the Russian people spoke and acted. They, too, took their chance to gain freedom, at least for a few years. Boris Yeltsin and the Russian people stood firm in Moscow and overthrew the Communist Party's domination of their country.

By Saturday the twenty-fourth of August the Russian people had destroyed the Communist Party's grip on their government. The Party's rule had led to the deaths of tens of millions, forty to sixty million people in all. No one can calculate the exact figure because Stalin and his successors destroyed so many 'unpleasant documents', as Stalin called them. But now the Party's rule was over, brought to an end by President Yeltsin and his supporters. Three young men died. The Patriarch of the Russian Orthodox Church conducted a solemn liturgy for their funerals. The procession stretched along the streets of Moscow, the people holding above their heads an unending white, blue and red flag, the flag of free Russia.

John Durham and his family watched it all on television and listened to all the radio reports. Soon the media in Britain would tire of these events; they would return to trivialities. But for a while there was a sense that something profound had happened. It was unwelcome to a surprisingly large number who, in one way or another, had placed a bet on 'Communism's bright future'. In politics and the media these people would work ceaselessly to try to make people forget that they had for so long echoed Soviet propaganda.

The timing of the collapse of the Communist party in the Soviet Union was unpredicted in the West. When he visited them in Battle on the Sunday after the funeral of the three young men, Geza told John and Giori that he and Miriam had heard from a friend at their synagogue that Pope John Paul II had expected it to happen soon, but he could not vouch for that story. Giori reminded them of what Geza had said to him during the Prague Spring in 1968, that it was those who seek goodness and truth, not power, who had such insight.

'Yes,' said Geza, quoting St Paul with his infectious zest, 'they are the ones who "have the mind of Christ".'

Stephen and Elizabeth knew that they had lived through one of the strangest weeks in the century.

'Will we meet Uncle Andrei *now*?' they asked impatiently.

'It was a miracle that brought the six of us together all those years ago, you know,' John said to Margaret. 'I can't believe it happened, really. I don't understand it. I didn't realise then how lucky we were. I was still so inexperienced a teacher, yet we managed to arrange one of the first school exchanges with Russia and Hungary; perhaps ours was the very first.

'Why did it happen to us at all? Perhaps it was because of the plans for Khrushchev's visit to London in the spring in 1956. I just feel so grateful; and so was your mother,' he added quietly.

Then, enthusiastically, John started talking to Stephen and Elizabeth about going to Moscow in the Christmas holidays, the visit for which he had longed for so many years, and which he and Barbara were never able to make together.

On that Sunday Andrei and Helena went for a cruise on a steamer on the Danube.

People will tell you that the 'Blue Danube' is really brown. It is smeared with oil, they say, from the tens of thousands of barges and tugs which use it as a canal, stretching through Central and Eastern Europe to its estuary on the Black Sea. Even the estuary, at one time so beautiful, is now just a drain, a sewer, with countless plastic bottles and polythene bags killing off the birds and fish. It may all be true, but on that Sunday morning in Budapest the River Danube did look blue for a while, reflecting a cloudless sky. By nine o'clock it was already hot.

The ship drifted along gently, past the Parliament building, steaming away from the massive, grotesque monument erected on Stalin's orders at the summit of a steep hill to mark the Red Army's victory over the Germans in Hungary in 1945.

An elegant Hungarian lady, with white hair, in her late sixties or seventies, gave a commentary to the tourists. Somehow it was incongruous that she was holding something as modern as a microphone, but she did so with grace. Most of the tourists that day were Hungarians, but the lady also spoke briefly in English and German.

'Now, after forty-six years, we can speak the whole truth,' she told the Westerners. 'That is because one month ago the last Soviet troops left our soil. For us, Hitler won the War in the shape of Stalin and his successors. It was the same in Poland, Bulgaria, Czechoslovakia, Yugoslavia, Romania, and East Germany... And now we are free.'

The guide closed her eyes and fell silent.

An hour later the boat pulled in at a quay on a large wooded island in the river. There was a cafe and a museum. The tourists drifted off towards them. Further away the congregation was coming out of church at the end of a service. The organ was playing a prelude by Bach.

Helena and Andrei went into the church. Their guide was already there, kneeling at prayer.

Andrei and Helena lit candles and crossed themselves and then they also prayed. After a few minutes they left and walked back towards the river cruiser. There was no one to be seen. The tourists and the crew were all drinking coffee; the guide was still in the church.

Now, at last, the moment had come. From her bag Helena took a small box. She did not know where Mother and Tibor lay. Nearly three thousand Hungarians had been killed in the uprising in 1956. Many of them lay in unmarked graves. Over half of those killed had been in their twenties or younger. About two hundred were under fourteen, younger even than Tibor when he had died.

Helena opened the box. From it she scattered into the Danube the earth and dust which Giori had scooped up and tied in a ball in his handkerchief and entrusted to her as they left Hungary as refugees.

'For you, Tibor; for you, Mother,' she said. 'We will not forget you.'

'I will never forget, Tibor,' said Andrei.

The guide left the church. She caught a glimpse of what Helena was doing. Perhaps she had seen such ceremonies before, for she did not question her or speak to her about it. There was sadness in her eyes, but she stood erect, as if in victory over some great evil that she had endured for over forty years, more than half her life, until its defeat. She had seen it through to its end. Now the truth about it could be told, but would people be interested for long? So quickly they became bored and forgot.

Gently, Andrei took Helena by the arm.

'Perhaps next summer we can go to Woody Bay,' he suggested, as they walked away. 'We might be able to get Margaret and Giori and John to come too.'

'Every year now,' replied Helena. 'For ever and ever...'

'For ever and ever,' said Andrei. 'It's not only when we are young that we can hope for that...'

Together, they walked back to the boat. It was all so different now. What had been so distant, even impossible, was real and very near. There was a lightness in the air.

'Terrible events,
unending danger...'

1905: October, constitutional changes, known as the First Russian Revolution, were made by Tsar Nikolai, with the beginnings of a Parliamentary democracy (the 'Duma'). From 1880 to 1914 the Russian economy grew rapidly.

1911: September, a terrorist murdered the Russian Prime Minister, Pyotr Stolypin. Other terrorist outrages occurred. The atmosphere of fear led to strict law and order measures. The hope of developing a peaceful democracy was deliberately extinguished by Lenin's Bolshevik Party and other extremist parties and terrorist groups.

1914: August, beginning of the First World War, with Austria-Hungary and Germany ranged against Serbia, Russia, Great Britain, France and later the United States of America.

1914-1917: Lenin, based outside Russia, received large sums of money from Imperial Germany to deploy the Bolsheviks in a campaign of agitation to demoralise the Russian people and the Army.

1914-1916: the fraudulent 'monk' Rasputin exploited the fears of Tsarina Alexandra (German by birth) for her son, a sufferer from haemophilia, and by his reputation for debauchery and corruption all but destroyed the standing of the Tsar's family among the Russian people of all classes.

1917: February, the Second Russian Revolution. Tsar Nikolai abdicated and his brother refused to accept the throne in his place. This marked the end of the three-hundred-year Romanov dynasty. A provisional government derived from the Duma exercised unsteady rule. It was heavily influenced by socialist extremists.

March, after his return to Russia in a train provided by Germany, Lenin and the Bolsheviks caused chaos. They attempted a *coup d'etat* in July.

October, Lenin and Trotsky led a successful *coup d'etat*, the so-called Third Russian Revolution.

1918: March, to secure Bolshevik power at any cost and to repay Germany for its support, Lenin signed the Treaty of Brest-Litovsk, ceding to Germany half of European Russia and taking Russia out of the First World War, deserting the Alliance against Germany.

July, the Tsar and his family were murdered by Bolsheviks in Siberia.

1918-1920: Russian Civil War, with at least thirteen million dead and two million exiles, amid famine and mass starvation.

1919-1920: temporary Communist *coups d'etat* in parts of Central and Eastern Europe, actively supported by Lenin and the Bolsheviks.

1920: 16th August, the Poles defeated the Soviet Army as it advanced on Warsaw to set up a Bolshevik government in Poland ('the miracle on the River Vistula'.)

1924: January, Lenin died. Over the next five years Stalin established his total power.

1920s: a series of weak Parliamentary governments in Germany, meeting in the city of Weimar and called the 'Weimar Republic', was undermined by the powerful German Communist Party acting on Stalin's orders out of enmity towards non-Communist socialists. Stalin thereby enhanced the rising power of Hitler and the National Socialists (the Nazis). Russia secretly helped Germany to re-arm in the 1920s and 1930s, against the terms of the Treaty of Versailles.

1929-1933: Between six and ten million Russian and Ukrainian peasant farmers died in Stalin's policy of 'collectivisation', depriving them of their small-holdings and forcing them into collective farms or exile in Siberia. There was devastating famine and mass starvation.

1933: 30th January, Hitler came to power.

1930-1953: Stalin's terror in the Soviet Union, including:

1936-1938: the so called Great Terror: many millions imprisoned and killed.

1939: August, a secret agreement was made in Moscow between Stalin and Hitler to divide Poland and the rest of Eastern Europe by invasions from east and west. Hitler and Stalin worked together as secret allies. It was an alliance of eventual enemies. Stalin's long-term aim was to seize control of Germany and its industrial power as a base for the conquest of Western Europe; Hitler's was to destroy Russia.

3rd September, Great Britain and France declared war on Germany two days after its attack on Poland. Two weeks later Stalin invaded Poland when Hitler's attack began to run into difficulties. Germany and Russia now had a common border in Poland.

1941: 21st June, Hitler attacked Russia to forestall an attack by Stalin on Germany. An alliance was formed between Great Britain and the USSR.

1941: 7th December, Japan attacked the US Navy at Pearl Harbour, Hawaii. Germany declared war on the US. The US joined the Alliance against Germany.

1945: May, defeat of Germany; August, defeat of Japan.

1945-1948: Stalin took power, by means of puppet regimes, in the states of Central and Eastern Europe, establishing the 'Iron Curtain' between East and West.

1949: The formation of the North Atlantic Treaty

Organisation (NATO) between the United States, Canada, Great Britain and West European countries.

1948-1949: Stalin blockaded West Berlin, which was saved by NATO's airlift of food and other vital supplies.

1950-1953: Communist North Korea, at Stalin's instigation and with the help of Soviet air power and Chinese Communist armies, attacked South Korea. The United Nations, under US leadership, fought the attack to a standstill.

1953: 5th March, Stalin died.

Short-lived disturbances occurred in several Eastern European countries, notably in East Germany, and in some parts of the GULAG.

1956: Hungary made an attempt to throw off Communism and Soviet control; crushed by invasion.

1961: August, the Soviet Union built a fortified wall in Berlin to divide East from West.

1962: Soviet operation to establish a nuclear base in Cuba to threaten the US.

1968: Czechoslovakia attempted to increase some freedoms while remaining Communist and staying in the Warsaw Pact alliance with the Soviet Union; crushed by invasion.

1960s and 1970s: severe repression continued in the Soviet Union and Eastern Europe, including the holding of political prisoners in psychiatric prisons and their torture. A great expansion of Soviet power and influence occurred in Asia, Africa and the Middle East.

1978: election of a Pole, Cardinal Karol Wojtyla, as Pope John Paul II.

1979: 31st December, Soviet invasion of Afghanistan.

1980-1983: the 'Solidarity' trade union movement swept Poland and martial law was imposed by the Polish Communist government. There was a widespread fear of Soviet invasion.

1969-1984: the Soviet Communist Party conspired with the German Social Democratic Party, in a clandestine liaison managed by the KGB, to devise a strategy to undermine Western Europe's support of the alliance with the US and to cause the United States to withdraw its forces from Western Europe and the dissolution of NATO. The strategy made 1983 one of the most dangerous times in the Cold War.

1984: Arthur Scargill, of the National Union of Mineworkers, fomented and exploited a miners' strike in Great Britain. Scargill received money from the Soviet Communist Party, authorized by Gorbachev, to advance his cause.

Early 1980s: growth of American and British determination, under President Reagan and Mrs Thatcher, weakening the Soviet Union, already afflicted by severe economic and social decay and political exhaustion.

1985: March, Mikhail Gorbachev's selection as Soviet leader by the Politburo of the Soviet Communist Party.

1989: Berlin Wall breached. Eastern and Central Europe freed itself from Soviet control.

1991: in the Soviet Union Gorbachev, backing away from his programme of reform and disowning those colleagues who had actively supported it, in alliance with hard-line Communists, reasserted repressive measures.

19th-24th August, the hard-line Communists finally over-reached themselves in a 'state *coup d'etat'*. President Yeltsin, by now the democratically elected leader of Russia, the largest of the fifteen Soviet republics, with great popular support, faced them down and outlawed the Communist Party of the Soviet Union because of its crimes at home and abroad. He started legal action against the leaders of the August coup, but, partly on the advice of Western governments, he did not pursue the cases and then pardoned them.

1992: the CPSU initiated proceedings in the Constitutional Court against President Yeltsin's prohibition of the Party. In November the Court ruled in the President's favour.

1993: Russian Communists regained influence in Parliament and forced President Yeltsin to modify his policies and change his prime minister. Russia lost its way in corruption and poverty.

1998 August, Russia defaulted on its foreign debts.

1998-1999: Putin became, successively, head of the Russian security service (formerly the KGB) in May 1998, Prime Minister in August 1999, and President at the end of December.

2000-2008: Putin was President. A steady return to authoritarian rule.

2008-2012: As Prime Minister, Putin controlled a puppet President, Medvedev, and changed the Constitution so as to be entitled by law to become President for two further terms.

2012: Putin resumed the Presidency.